A Killing in
San Geronimo

When Jack Malpas stepped of the stage in San Geronimo it was meant to be a new beginning. Left for dead in the epic gun battle that had destroyed the Butler gang, his marshalling days had seemed over. But it wasn't to work out that way.

Despite its sleepy, Spanish-style air, San Geronimo is anything but. Malpas quickly finds himself searching for the kidnapped newspaper heiress Susan Hauksbee, first with a posse and then alone in New Mexico. With the odds stacked so high against him, has Malpas a hope in hell of winning through?

A Killing in
San Geronimo

MIKE STALL

A Black Horse Western

ROBERT HALE · LONDON

ISBN-10: 0-7090-8049-2
ISBN-13: 978-0-7090-8049-7

Robert Hale Limited
Clerkenwell House
Clerkenwell Green
London EC1R 0HT

Typeset by Derek Doyle & Associates, Shaw Heath
Printed and bound in Great Britain by
Antony Rowe Limited, Wiltshire

for E. L.

PROLOGUE

Marshal Jack Malpas was sitting comfortably, his feet on the office desk, when he heard the shots. He swore silently. It was a quiet Monday and his deputy wasn't coming to relieve him for an hour yet, when he was expected to to go and meet with the mayor. Well maybe he wouldn't be meeting him today.

He stood up, checked the gun on his hip and the derringer in his jacket pocket, then glanced at the weapons rack, finally selecting a Greener shotgun. He took some spare shells too, then walked to the door.

He saw the horses hitched no to the rail outside the bank – four of them, horses he'd never seen before. Likewise the man standing by them holding a Henry rifle.

The situation was clear. Somebody had chosen to break the peace of a quiet Monday by robbing the bank – not the most lucrative, but perhaps the safest time to do it. And what to do about that Henry rifle? Go back and fetch a Winchester instead?

No. And suddenly he was moving, keeping close to the shadowed wall, getting into range. At odds of four to one he needed the shotgun, and to get close enough to use it effectively.

The man watching over the horses saw him when he was a good thirty yards off, and fired. Malpas flung himself forward; the bullet went nowhere near him. He set the Greener down beside him and drew his six-gun. He took quick but careful aim, then fired. The robber's second shot went skywards as he crumpled down on to the wooden sidewalk.

Malpas was on his feet in an instant and moving forward. There was no back entrance to the bank for security's sake. If he got near enough with the Greener, the odds would be on his side.

He could have hung back, fought it out with a carbine in relative safety but, if he had, the robbers would have got away with the town's money and that was just what they paid him to keep from happening.

He was within twenty yards of the bank when the three of them came out – in a bunch and shooting. Malpas, the Greener still in his left hand, felt the bullets from their six-guns crack past him. He raised his own and fired back, emptying the cylinder.

He saw one of the three fall even as he was holstering his own gun. He switched to the Greener, cocking and firing it at the remaining pair. One of the men was flung back by the force of the impact but the other was scarely harmed. Malpas scrabbled in his pocket for fresh shells, but the remaining man had plucked a Henry rifle from the saddle sheath of one of the terrified horses and now he was aiming it at him.

Crack! Malpas felt a pain in his left leg as if a hammer had hit it. He still rammed the shells home and closed up the Greener. He was cocking it when the bullet smashed into it and tore it from his grip, leaving his right hand numb and useless.

Crack! He felt the pain in his side instantly. His knees gave and he fell forward on to them. And then the fourth man was there, just a dozen feet away, looking down on him.

'You killed my brothers, you damned lawdog!' he yelled, raising the Henry but not firing it. He was obviously going to draw out his revenge.

Malpas slipped his hand into the left pocket of his jacket, cocked and fired the derringer through the cloth. The slow, heavy bullet took the bank robber in the sternum, smashing through it and his backbone. He pitched backwards, arms flung out, and collapsed on the sidewalk. But Mabpas had no time to savour his victory. He found himself falling forward into the dark.

ONE

I

Malpas awoke and found himself looking at a strange ceiling. It was made of white painted planks and there was a big oil lamp suspended from it, not lit now as the light was streaming in from a window opposite him. All he could see out of it from his bed was the roof of O'Leary's saloon, which meant he was in the upper storey of Doc Crosbie's place. It made sense.

He tried to move. His limbs seemed to work but very reluctantly; his left leg most of all. He made no attempt to get out of bed. Anyway, he doubted he could, not yet. He'd taken three slugs from a Henry rifle and he was lucky to be alive. He was in for a few days of bed rest.

And something to eat. He felt very hungry and even thristier, as if—

The door opened and Doc Crosbie, an old man in an older-fashioned suit, entered.

'Ah, we're awake,' he said.

'I am,' Malpas said. 'You speak for yourself.' But his voice sounded dry and crackly.

'Good, good, we retain a sense of humour,' Crosbie said, with the weariness of a man who'd heard all the jokes many times before. 'How do we feel?'

'Weak,' Malpas admitted.

'That's inevitable. You've been in a fever for quite a while.'

Cosbie's vagueness prompted Malpas to ask, 'How long?'

'Ten days.'

Malpas let out his breath, then: 'How bad is it?'

'It could have been a lot worse. The shot to the leg tore the muscle but missed bone and artery. The second shot broke your hand but there was no penetration. The shot to your side was the problem. As far as I can tell it missed everything vital – the kidneys, the liver and the stomach – but introduced quite a bit of foreign matter, mostly from your jacket and shirt. I cleared it all out as best I could but that caused the problem. It was touch and go but you seem to be out of it now.'

Malpas didn't like what he was hearing. 'How long before I'm up and around, Doc?'

'Give it a few days before you even try. In the meantime, you should eat. I'll get Mrs McGee to bring up a tray.'

Mrs McGee was his housekeeper, practical nurse and – if gossip were to be believed – his mistress.

'I'll be OK though, Doc?'

'It could have been a lot worse,' Crosbie said, and departed.

That meant it could have been better. Malpas forced a smile. He'd been shot before and the doctors had never been cheerful. He'd survived, nevertheless.

He forced himself up into a sitting position. It was hard work and left him sweating after the effort. He ached all over and his side felt as if there were a knife in there. And his right hand was unrecognizable, bound tight in leather to immobilize it, making it a virtually useless club. But it didn't hurt at all.

II

He didn't see Crosbie again for three days. There was a difficult confinement out on the north range and he was the only doctor in fifty miles. But Mrs McGee fed and watered him and his strength grew. He tried to get information out of her but she made it clear that prognoses were Crosbie's business, not hers.

'You just eat your victuals and get your strength up,' was all she would come up with by way of answer, except that the reasons no visitors ever came was because Crosbie had forbidden them.

Local news was a different matter. The robbers had been the Butler gang, four brothers out of East Texas, all gone bad. And not only had he killed them all, he'd saved the town sixteen thousand dollars by doing it. 'You deserve a medal, Marshal Malpas,' she said.

He didn't reply. He already had one from the war and precious little good had it ever done him.

Finally, the indignity of being an invalid was too much for him. He decided to walk to the window.

He almost fell getting out of bed. He stood a moment, sweating profusely, weak as a kitten. Twelve steps, he estimated. He could manage a measly twelve steps.

It was the hardest, longest journey of his life. His left leg hurt like the devil and the pain in his side was, if anything, worse. And worst of all was that he seemed to have no reserves left, just weakness behind weakness. But somehow he managed it and stood at last leaning on the wall beside the window and looking out.

The town seemed no different. Coopersville, West Texas, in all its glory: the same dusty Main Street with its raised, wooden sidewalks; the same mix of adobe and timberframe buildings with just the bank and jail built of bricks. People passed but no one looked up. Why should they? Had he ever cared about who was in Crosbie's upper-room?

Then the rig drew up directly below with Crosbie driving and he decided to get back to his bed. It was a little easier this time, but not much. He sat on the bed in his nightshirt, utterly drained.

Crosbie didn't linger downstairs. 'Ah, I see we've been out and about. Well, let's see the damage.'

After a quick examination, Crosbie stood back. 'No harm done, so it appears. How do you feel?'

'Lousy.'

'That's to be expected. In all, I'd say quite satisfactory. A few days more and you'll be properly mobile.'

'What about my hand?' Malpas asked, waving the club hand in the air.

'Two weeks and more isn't long, but the binding was precautionary. I'll have a look.' He dug out a large clasp knife from his pocket and said, 'You can lie down.'

Malpas stuck out his hand, staying as he was.

'As you will, as you will,' Crosbie said and set to work.

Crosbie seemed satisfied. 'I really ought to bind it up again but if you don't put pressure on it . . .'

So it had been sprained, rather than broken, Malpas realized, though Crosbie wasn't about to admit that.

'Now, move your fingers individually.'

16

Malpas did so. There was no strength in them but they worked. 'Now the thumb.'

The base of it worked but above the joint didn't. It was an amazing thing to will it to move and for it not to.

'Let's see that,' Crosbie said, feeling it with his fingers. 'Nothing broken, no damage at all. It must be the nerve.'

'So I'll get it back working soon?'

Crosbie stood back, scratched his chin. 'If the damage was slight, it should have repaired itself in two weeks. It hasn't, so I'd say not. But I'm just a country sawbones.'

Malpas knew Crosbie was speaking the truth as he saw it. And without proper use of his thumb he couldn't draw and cock a Colt six-gun. His days as a marshal were over.

III

Dale Ivory was the first of his visitors and, significantly, he wasn't wearing his deputy marshal's badge. He was properly cheerful, but there was an undertone of apology in his manner. Malpas made nothing of it, merely asking him to fetch his clothes from his hotel room. 'Sure thing,' Dale said and left.

The rest of them skirted similarly around the fact that their marshal was now an invalid. Then it was Mayor Daley's turn, two days after Ivory's visit. Malpas met him downstairs in Crosbie's parlour, dressed in his second best suit – his best being now full of holes – with his badge on it. He couldn't help but notice how Daley's eyes were drawn to the badge.

'Good to see you up and about, Jack. I want to express the whole council's appreciation for what you did. There was a reward for the Butler gang amounting to five hundred dollars. Of course we've applied for that on your behalf and more than that, we're matching it ourselves.' He brought out a cheque from his pocket. 'This is for a thousand dollars. Please accept it with our gratitude.'

Malpas took the cheque and glanced over it. It was hardly riches but still much more than most of the small ranchers hereabouts saw in a lifetime. Together with the eight hundred dollars savings already in his account, it was enough to buy a small business and potter about town on the proceeds.

He said, 'What did Crosbie tell you about me?'

'Well—'

'Spit it out, Mayor!'

Daley grimaced, then: 'That you'll be a semi-invalid for quite a while and that you'll never draw a Colt and fire it again.'

'So you want this badge,' Malpas said. And after a moment's silence he plucked it from his jacket and tossed it to Daley. 'I know you've appointed Dale Ivory anyway.'

'He wasn't supposed to—'

'Tell me? He didn't. But he didn't wear his deputy's badge either. Why not? I asked myself. The answer was obvious. He wasn't a deputy anymore.'

'You have to see our position—' Daley began.

'No, I don't have to,' Malpas said. 'But Crosbie's right. I can't shoot worth a damn. It's time to move on.'

Daley sighed with relief. Then: 'Where to?'

Malpas hadn't considered the matter, hadn't made his decision until the instant before. 'California,' he said. That was where all trails ended.

'Good luck to you out there, Jack. You can

be assured—'

Malpas interrupted him by handing back the cheque. 'Get that cashed for me; a thousand in gold and the rest of my account in bills. I'll pay Doc Crosbie.'

'No,' Daley said, 'the town will do that, and your hotel bill. It'll be free and clear.'

Malpas suddenly realized there was more to it all than just his infirmity. Four men gunned down in the street was the wrong image for a growing township, especially if the man who had shot them was still there, advertising the fact.

'We're grateful, very grateful,' Daley said, and offered his hand.

Malpas hesitated, then offered his left. Maybe Daley wasn't altogether wrong. Who really needed gun battles in the street? Hell, this was the nineteenth century after all.

IV

Crosbie had been none too pleased to lose his patient – he was still too weak, etc. Well, maybe he was but Malpas knew Crosbie saw him as an invalid and nothing more. Crosbie was no further use to him.

By way of parting gifts Crosbie had presented him with a thumb-sized leather fingerstall and a broad, two-buckle wrist protector. He'd thanked him, intending to discard at least the fingerstall, maybe using the wrist protector for a while. He walked over to the hotel to collect his things – very little – and then on to the livery stable. The few people he met were effusive but embarrassed. Malpas was unsurprised. He was just a shabby ghost of the man he used to be, at least for now.

At the livery his friend Harry Cryper was glad to see him. 'Hell, you look awful.'

'I feel worse,' MaInas said, smiling. 'Now, sell me a horse.'

'What for?'

'Riding west.'

'Hell, are you—'

'Leaving? Yes.'

'Hell, are you—'

'Up for it? Who knows? I'm going to do it anyway. If I stay, Crosbie'll turn me into a full-time invalid and, if you hadn't notieed, I don't have a job any longer.'

'That was—'

'Understandable,' Malpas said, not wanting to get into it all again. He held up his right hand, the dark leather stall on his thumb prominent. 'I can't cock a gun quickly anymore.'

Cryper nodded. 'I heard tell.' He paused. 'I was reading some time back how some Englishman had made a handgun you didn't have to cock – Adams, that was his name. The pull on the trigger itself cocks the gun.'

'Yeah,' Malpas said, vaguely remembering something about it. 'What's the catch?'

'There's movement in the mechanism as you fire but . . .'

'Beggars can't be choosers,' Malpas completed for him. 'Where could I get one?'

'Not here. McCulloch stocks little else but Colts. Maybe Squire in San Geronimo – hell, almost for sure. He prides himself on having that kind of thing. But it's a heck of a long ride through the mountains.'

But a short one through the desert, Malpas thought. He might as well have spoken out loud for Cryper saw it in his eyes.

'The Little Stony Desert is a killer for fit men. It would . . .' Cryper broke off.

'Kill a cripple?' Malpas laughed. 'Well,

maybe that's what I need. Kill or cure.'

Cryper obviously wanted to argue but seeing it would be no use, he yielded. 'It's your life, Jack. God willing, things will work out.' Then he picked him a horse, the one called Swifty because he was anything but, though he was strong, faithful and tough as nails. He fetched Malpas's saddle and an old but serviceable waterbag.

'I'll see to things,' he said, handing Malpas a cigar. 'You go out back and smoke that. And you can leave your gold with me.'

That Harry Cryper knew of it wasn't surprising. He was a councilman too. Why he wanted it was another matter but Malpas didn't ask. He trusted Cryper absolutely. He handed over the gold and went out back to smoke the cigar, his first in getting on for a month. It was a cheap, nickel cigar but it still tasted good. After a while he went back inside.

Swifty was ready and the saddle-bags were stuffed out with more than his few clothes. He looked to Cryper.

'I put some coffee, beans and bacon in 'em,' Cryper said. Then he handed him a gunbelt, a fancy one in black leather but with Malpas's own gun in it.

'You'd best wear this.'

'Why? I can't draw and fire.'

'It's for a left-handed gun. Wear it with the buckle at the back and you can draw and fan the damn thing if you have to.'

Malpas laughed but put it on, switching it about as described. He didn't attempt a draw. He knew how slow he was with his left.

'One more thing: you're forgetting your money.' He reached for a money-belt, which had been hung on the saddlehorn on the side away from Malpas, and tossed it to him. Malpas caught it with his left hand, felt the weight of the gold in it and then put it on over his shirt.

'I can hide it later.' He smiled. 'If I'd been wearing this then, I'd be one bullet lighter.'

'Yeah,' Cryper said.

'How much do I—'

'Jack, I'd money in that bank. There were other times too. Much more than that, you're my friend. Take it, it's a gift.' He paused. 'Hell, Swifty ain't much anyhow.' He offered his hand. Malpas took it, risking his own right.

They walked out front, Cryper leading the horse for him. Mounting was bad. His left leg pained him considerably as he lifted himself into the saddle but he managed it. He nodded to his friend, set off down Main Street, heading west.

Nobody in Coopersville paid him any attention.

TWO

I

From Coopersville to the edge of the Little Stony was a three-day ride; two if you pushed it. Malpas took seven. On the first night he slept under the stars and woke up cold, stiff and weary. The second he spent at a small ranch he'd come upon, paying for his supper and a palliasse of straw in the barn. The rancher asked six bits but Malpas haggled him down to four, having seen something in his eyes. If he'd thought his guest had money there was a possibility that guest wouldn't wake from his sleep, at least in this world.

All the same, it was a useful lesson. He was no longer the redoubtable Marshal Malpas;

now he was just another saddle tramp, one with a limp and a crippled hand. He'd get no favours he didn't pay for. Kids would no longer call him 'sir' nor adults defer to him in any way. It was all the harsher because he felt no different inside, but it was a lesson that had to be learnt and learnt well. The following night he slept again under the stars with his gun under the blanket near his left hand.

On the fourth day he tried out his shooting, drawing crosswise with his left and fanning with his right. It proved a good way of wasting ammunition. He hit a man-sized rock twenty feet off only three times out of twelve. He could learn to do better but for the time being it seemed better to save his bullets.

By the seventh day he was sore and tired but the ache in his leg had dulled and his torn innards seemed well on the way to healing fully. He had strength back in his fingers but not in his thumb which, almost despite himself, he kept in the leather stall, as if in disgrace.

It was then that he came to the farmstead and a surprise – sheep. They were scrawny, Mexican-style sheep though the shepherd wasn't. His name was Billy Mapes and he had the air of an old man though he was probably no older than fifty.

'How do I keep from getting myself shot, you wonder?' Mapes said. 'Truth is, nobody cares much about sheep hereabouts. Folks wonder how anything can live on land so barren and, truth to tell, a leg of mutton's welcome in most nearby ranches if only for the change.'

Mapes welcomed him into his decrepit, adobe house and asked for no payment. Malpas decided he could trust him, within limits.

There was no lamb on the menu. Mapes had already done his slaughtering and selling two weeks back and it was just beans and coffee with some pan-baked bread. 'Hell, I don't get visitors often. Maybe I ought to whet my knife and—'

'No, not for me,' Malpas said. 'This is fine, much appreciated.'

'You're a gentleman, sir. I reckon you was in the war too, an officer likely enough.'

Malpas admitted as much.

'And now you've hit hard times, like me. Heck, I didn't set out to be a shepherd though I wouldn't change it now. Sheep are pretty amiable critters if'n you make allowances. No, the way it happened was . . .'

Malpas listened politely, not very interested, saying 'yes' and 'no' here and there as seemed appropriate. It crossed his mind that he to could end up like Mapes, maybe not a shepherd but half-lost nevertheless, and then he dismissed the idea. He wasn't like Mapes nor ever could be.

'So you'll be going south tomorrow,' Mapes said when the meal was over.

'No, I'm going across the desert.'

Mapes's eyes widened. 'There's few as do that.'

'I'm going to San Geronimo. It's the quickest route, I'm told. Have you crossed it?'

Mapes shook his head. 'Never cared to try. It's a nasty place, believe me. It ain't little and it's not altogether stony either. Halfway across there's the salt flats. Very nasty indeed, so I've heard. And then there's Sharp Ridge to cross before you get to the San Geronimo road. I'd think again, sir.'

'No, I'm set on it,' Malpas said.

He slept on old sacking before the fire, slept well, and awoke to find bread and coffee awaiting him. Again Mapes tried to dissuade him, recognized his failure and helped him to fill the waterbag and the canteen, also giving what advice he could, the gist of it being not to cross the salt flats in the heat of the day.

Malpas pressed two dollars into his hand, unasked, and half-regretted it as he rode off. Maybe he should have accepted the hospitality as freely as it was given. Then again, maybe that would have been mean. Two dollars would buy half a dozen bottles of mescal to help pass the empty nights.

II

The first day of the crossing was easy enough. There was scrub and rock enough, but too scattered to impede a rider – or a man leading a horse, for every hour Malpas dismounted and led Swifty to spell him a while.

By noon, Swifty was still fresh but Malpas wasn't. He was sweating and nauseous and aching in every limb. It seemed as if the Little Stony would be more kill than cure.

He found some shade in the lee of a tall rock and let Swifty graze as best he could on the end of a long line. This still wasn't totally plantless desert – they'd come to that – and

Swifty seemed quite content. Malpas didn't eat, smoking one of the cigars Cryper had gifted him with in the saddle-bags. After a while he felt better. It was hot and dry but so much the better. It would sweat the last of the fever and weakness out of him.

He nooned for two hours, his mind going back to the war, something he hadn't thought of in years. He'd come through everything without a scratch, by the end of it leading a company of men he scarcely knew because the ones he had known were all gone, killed in petty skirmishes or major charges, or taken off screaming to the surgeons to die of gangrene or survive as cripples. He'd pitied them briefly, then put them out of mind because there was a job to be done. And now it was his turn.

He smiled grimly. It wasn't over yet. He'd uncripple himself or die in the attempt. He glanced at the stall on his thumb. Maybe even crossing the Little Stony wouldn't affect that but in San Geronimo he'd buy himself one of the new fangled double-action guns and solve the problem differently. All he had to do was get there. He stood up. Dark thoughts solved nothing. The job had to be done.

III

It took two days to get to the salt flats and by then he was very near total exhaustion. Even Swifty was tired and the water was half used up. It was three hours off dark and he was tempted to sleep through the night but he knew he couldn't risk it by daylight. Nor could he risk sleeping for a couple of hours because he was certain he'd not wake in time. Instead he watered Swifty and cleaned him up as best he could in the absence of a curry comb and then cooked the last of the bacon – beans he could do without.

Night fell yielding up the stars and he set course by them, though it was unnecessary. All he really needed to do was to ride west and he'd get through. He saddled up Swifty, mounted. He'd already decided to ride without interruption on the salt, which would be easier going for the horse than for him – and the sooner they were past it, the better. Getting caught out there in the sun wasn't a good idea.

The going was easy at first; the salt wasn't thick, no more than a few inches – the detritus of some dried up lake – and it was even and harder than sand on the surface. But after about two hours Swifty showed signs of real weariness so, despite his intentions, he dismounted and set out to lead the horse.

During the war, the men had sometimes sung as they walked their horses – not battle hymns but the popular songs of the day. By the end of it they no longer sang. I ought to sing now, he thought, but his throat was too parched and salty – it was in the air you breathed – and besides, the words and music were mostly lost to him. He tried hard to remember just one song but while odd phrases came to him, he couldn't recall what followed, and the only rhythm that came back to him was the plodding rhythm of men and horses.

Sometime in the night, he fell. He couldn't remember falling, only lying there with Swifty nuzzling him, his great nostrils dry and salt-caked.

Was it lighter? How long had he slept there in the salt? But he couldn't recall that either. He struggled to his feet, tried to lead the horse forward but there was no strength left in him.

'It's up to you now, boy,' he said, somehow pulling himself aboard, and sat there with the reins in his hands trying to stop himself swaying in the saddle. Using the stirrups might help there, he thought to himself, and it did, a little.

He must have slept in the saddle, for one moment it was night and then it was day, the sun low in the east casting long shadows ahead of them. Swifty was still plodding on, and amazingly he could see the end of the flats.

He rubbed his salt-rimmed eyes, looked again. Yes just three or four hundred yards and the white salt expanse gave way to dark rock. He was tempted to ride there but halted his horse.

'We'll walk together, boy,' he said, dismounting. 'Oats for you in San Geronimo, and all the hay you can eat. You're a good old horse, Swifty, a good old horse.'

Swifty ignored his ravings but started again when he did and they moved forward. His legs were scarcely any better but by a supreme effort of will he placed one foot in front of the other and kept going. The ache in his left leg was lost now, subsumed in a dozen others, but he set them all aside as unworthy of notice. Just reaching that black line where salt ended and rock began was all that mattered.

At last they made it. He wanted very badly to sleep but forced himself to unsaddle Swifty and water him after wiping away the salt incrustations. He took some of the water himself but only a little – he was too tired even to be thirsty. Only then did he let himself lie down on the ground and sleep.

But not for long. He awoke even before it was full noon. The heat was rolling upon them from the salt flats which, when he looked, seemed more like a great expanse of molten metal, and despite himself he shuddered at the thought of being caught out there at noon-day.

He saddled Swifty and led him onwards. The ground was now too broken to think of riding, and even the rocks were growing warm under-foot. Ahead, he could see Sharp Ridge as a dark strip separating land and sky, but even after an hour's walk it appeared no nearer and Swifty was growing clumsy from tiredness. Or maybe hunger and thirst. What had seemed shared before he now realized was only imposed: his will on the horse. He was the one driving on for his own purposes. And the horse needed rest.

Almost as soon as he thought that, he saw it in the lee of a great rock: a small garden, a tiny oasis without open water but with grass almost too green to look at. It had to survive on the dew from the rock itself.

Swifty snuffed the air, became firmer footed and soon they were there and he rapidly stripped off bridle and saddle and let the horse have his freedom to graze. He used that same saddle to pillow his sleep in the much needed shade of the rock itself, for the sun had now reached its zenith.

But he didn't exactly sleep. Maybe he was too weary for sleep, maybe he would never sleep again, just go on for ever getting wearier and wearier but never able to – No, that was nonsense. A dark thought. A foolish thought. They were almost there. A few more hours and they'd reach the ridge and the San Geronimo road beyond it. There'd be time for sleep there, as before. He only wished he had a cigar left, even the horrible nickel cigars Cryper favoured. He—

Swifty screamed. Malpas had heard horses scream before, in battle and after, but this was even more piercing. He shook himself out of his doze and saw the horse bucking at the other side of the lost garden . . . and hanging from its flank something long and green.

A snake, a rock viper or some kind of rattler.

His first thought was to shoot it off but that was impossible now. He ran towards the horse, cross-drawing and reversing the six-gun to use it as a club, but the snake had already loosened its grip. It fell free and slithered quickly back into the mess of rock at the side of the garden. He didn't even get the chance to reverse the gun again and get a left-handed shot off at it.

He turned to Swifty, calm now but still wild-eyed. 'Easy, boy,' he said, reaching out to touch his neck. 'Calm's better. It may not have been poisonous.' But it was a lie, he knew, and one made even more ludicrous by being told to a horse. 'Let's see the wound.'

Amazingly, Swifty stood still when he tried to suck out the venom and spit it out, but all he could taste was blood. Maybe. . . .

The venom began its work in minutes. Swifty frothed at the mouth, his eyes rolling and soon he could no longer stand. Convulsions followed.

'Forgive me, boy,' Malpas said. The horse turned its head and saw the gun in his hand. It turned away. Cocking the gun with his right palm, he pulled the trigger. He fired a second shot to be sure. And Swifty lay still.

Clumsily, Malpas holstered the gun. Maybe

he would have wept if the moisture hadn't been leached out of him, and after a moment he cursed his own stupidity. It should have been obvious that this place would be a haven for snakes. There would be many others. If he'd slept, he too would have died. By his death, Swifty had saved his life.

Checking carefully, he culled what he couldn't carry – saddle, bridle and the waterbag, though filling his canteen first. Then, saddlebags over his shoulder, with one backward glance at the horse, he departed this paradise of serpents.

Night came with his arrival at the ridge but it didn't stop him. The stars were bright and it was no feat to climb its steep, lightly turfed slopes. There were no rocks to impede him, long since washed down by forgotten rains or set rolling by the winds that had made the Little Stony Desert in the first place.

In an hour he stood on the height of the ridge and looked down on the plain stretching out west, only sporadically sketched in by the starlight. Somewhere out there was the road to San Geronimo.

Perhaps he ought to wait the night out here.

There would be no snakes, not where the wind from the west would leach the heat out of their cold-blooded bodies. And he was at the end of his strength. But he had been that for days and he knew he wasn't going to stop. He'd do that when he got to the road and not before.

THREE

I

'Hey, mister!'

Somebody was prodding him. He opened his eyes, saw a small boy in home-made garments reaching out towards him with a bare foot.

'You ain't dead?' The boy sounded almost disappointed.

'Even dead, I wouldn't care to be kicked,' Malpas said. He glanced up at the sky. It was well after noon. It had just been turning light when he'd found the road – no more than stage ruts in the sandy soil – and let himself sleep twenty yards off it.

'I didn't kick you,' the boy said, pulling his foot back.

'No doubt,' Malpas agreed.

'You talk funny. Where you from?'

'I just came across the desert.' And he saw the boy believed him. Why not? He had to look like a man who'd crossed the desert.

He asked, 'Where are you from?'

'The relay station.'

'The stage relay station?'

'Sure thing.'

'Where is it?'

'Just up the road, behind the rocks there.' The boy pointed. 'You want to go on the stage?'

'Yes.'

'Where?'

'San Geronimo.'

'Got dollars for it?'

Malpas smiled at the outspokenness of the child. He had to look like a scarecrow so why should he have dollars? The kid couldn't guess he had a thousand dollars in gold around his waist and nearly as much sewn into the lining of his jacket. He'd also some loose money in his pockets, enough for a meal and a stage line ticket.

'I've got a few,' he said.

'Come on, I'll lead the way.'

So he got to his feet and made his way to the relay station led by a whooping and dancing boy.

II

Bert Gilett ran the relay station. It wasn't elaborate: it consisted of a house, a barn and a corral and nothing more, and the house parlour had also to serve as a refreshment room for the passengers, if they wanted it. Mostly they didn't.

San Geronimo was less than a day's ride off and if the journey from the north hadn't been all on a rise, there'd have been no reason to use fresh stock. As it was, he had less than a dozen horses, which was too few, but the bosses of the stage line took no account of him. Why should they? Nobody else did.

'Pa, Pa!' Willy shouted. Bert Gilett looked up from the bridle he was mending and saw his son coming round the bend, followed at some distance by a tall, gaunt figure in a dark, ragged suit.

'He's crossed the desert, Pa! I found him by the road.'

42

Bert smiled, not exactly in belief, but as they drew nearer he looked at the stranger and saw the strain in his face, the sallowness . . . and something else in the eyes, a total indomitability. This was a man who could cross the desert and live to tell of it.

'Welcome, friend,' he said. 'Come into the house. We'll get some victuals into you.'

The vituals turned out to be oven-baked bread, beans and coffee to wash them down with. Malpas guessed it was their staple diet.

'I hope you can pay for this, stranger,' Mrs Gilett said. She was a hard-faced woman, about thirty but already her skin was wrinkling and there was tiredness about her eyes. She'd lived a hard life and there were no prospects of ease to come. Running a relay station wasn't much of a job, even with the bigger lines, and the Dwight Line, which this was, seemed to be a pretty rickety business.

'Yes, ma'am, I pay my way. For this and a bed somewhere. Your husband tells me the stage isn't due till tomorrow morning.'

'We ain't got no spare beds, mister. We ain't no hotel. But you can sleep in here with some clean blankets.'

'I'm obliged, ma'am,' he said, digging into

his beans. He could see she was itching to talk money but he didn't want to haggle with her. Anyway, her husband was the station manager, not her. As if suddenly realizing this she disappeared into the kitchen leaving him alone in the big parlour-cum-refreshment room.

The beans were as poorly cooked as the bread and the coffee wasn't made from fresh grounds but he left nothing, and had to restrain himself from asking for seconds.

Malpas awoke late when the family had already been moving around for quite a time. He pushed off the blankets and stood up. The big parlour clock, with the plaque that announced it was the property of the Dwight Line, also told him the time: 8.30. The stage was due in little over an hour and it suddenly crossed his mind that he hadn't washed in quite a while. Hot water? There wasn't time. He begged a bucket and soap and repaired to the barn with his saddle-bags.

Asking Gilett, who was working outside, to act as guardian of the door he had a stand up bath, drying himself on an undershirt. He found a spare one, and a shirt too, in the bags and dressed himself afresh. There were also

44

spare trousers which he put on, but his jacket couldn't be replaced; besides, it had the money in it. But he brushed it halfway to respectability. He next cleaned his hat with the improvised towel and then his boots. Finally, he ran his hand over his face. Shave? No, he had difficulties shaving himself and his beard was long enough to be respectable though he'd get it shaved off when he arrived in San Geronimo. Satisfied, he took bucket and soap outside.

'You look a hell of a lot better,' Bert Gilett said.

Oddly enough, he felt much better too though he hadn't realized it until that moment.

'It's three bucks to town,' Gilett added. 'Don't let Coleman stiff you.' He paused, them added, 'You've forgotten your gunbelt.'

Malpas found he had. Odd to forget that. He went back in to collect it but he held it rather than put it on. He knew he still had difficulty with buckles for in the privacy of the barn he'd wondered if the feeling better had extended itself to that be-stalled member. It hadn't.

III

Coleman had tried it on – he'd asked for seven dollars and failed. Malpas was glad he'd given Gilett five bucks with the proviso he didn't mention his guest had come out of the Little Stony. It would get out eventually but he preferred to avoid publicity. Marshal Malpas had had enemies that Jack Malpas could no longer be sure of dealing with. He'd also given young Willy his change – nearly a dollar in nickels and dimes and seen the near awe in his face. Not that he reckoned he'd keep hold of them for long. Mrs Gilett would confiscate them and use them to buy beans. But such was life. He looked around at his fellow passengers. The man on his left had the look of preacher and was probably an undertaker. Opposite left was a large, fat man in a well pressed serge suit. And directly opposite was a very handsome young woman reading a black bound book; not an easy occupation in the poorly sprung coach. She glanced up at him nervously, looked back in her book. He suddenly realized she'd been looking at the gunbelt on his lap. He quickly put it between him and the side of the coach, the grip upwards and the barrel pointing back and down.

'My apologies, ma'am,' he said.

'It was no matter,' she said formally.

'You reckoned to hold off the James gang, young fella?' the fat man said and laughed. 'Nobody told you we ain't carrying a strong-box?'

Malpas ignored him, concentrated instead on reading the title of the book: *Selected Poems of Percy B. Shelley*. She noticed him doing it and looked up.

'You admire Shelley, sir?'

'No, ma'am,' he said. 'Not as a man . . . and as a poet even less.'

'So who is your favourite poet?'

It was a bizarre conversation and the only way to handle it was truthfully, except he'd always favoured Horace though he hadn't read him in years and probably no longer could. He temporized: 'I'd say Pope, ma'am.'

She smiled, surprised a little. She obviously hadn't expected to come across even a half-educated travelling companion on a stage line journey.

'Pshaw, poets!' the fat man said. 'Danged effeminate fools the lot of 'em!'

'I'll ask you to mind your language, sir,' the preacher/undertaker said. 'There's a lady present.'

'You needn't worry, Mr Thorogood, I'm an emancipated young woman.'

Which meant she certainly wasn't, Malpas thought. The ones who were ... well, he'd heard up Wyoming way there was talk of giving women the vote in state elections. He wondered why they wanted it. In the end all you came up with was a politician.

'Do you dislike Keats too?' she asked.

'No, ma'am,' Malpas said, thinking it wise to profess a moderate admiration for the gentleman. Happily she didn't pursue the matter once the point was made and they talked pleasantly of more mundane affairs. She tried to bring them all into the conversation, not very successfully. Mr Thorogood, whom Malpas was now quite sure was an undertaker, did his best and contributed a few stilted commonplaces, while the fat man just sulked and it was back to just the two of them.

He learnt that she had inherited a newspaper in San Geronimo and that she had been educated back East. She learnt that he was travelling on business. Fortunately she wasn't very interested in just what business it was.

After a while she smiled at him and picked up the book again. Malpas looked politely out of the glassless window through the dust kicked up by the wheels at the dusty landscape beyond. Occasionally he glanced back at her. He'd been quite wrong in his initial estimation, he decided. She was more than handsome. She was quite lovely.

And then the coach drew up in a dusty town and she was leaving.

'Goodbye, gentlemen,' she said as she was stepping out of the stage coach, aided by a huge, florid-faced man in his early forties who had obviously been waiting for her.

Suddenly she was out of his life forever. He didn't even know her name.

Mr Thorogood would know it, he thought. He only had to ask. But he didn't. The florid man hadn't been her father or any relation. He'd seen the way he looked at her, and she had taken his arm as they walked away. She hadn't looked back.

It was then he noticed she'd left something behind – the black bound book. He reached across and took it, opened it. Not for the poems but the opening page. A name was there:

'Susan Hauksbee.'

'I'll take that,' Thorogood said, getting out of his seat. 'I'll see it gets to her.'

Malpas handed it to him wordlessly. At least now he had a name to put to her face. It would do him no good but it was still nice to know it.

He was the last out of the coach. Coleman threw him his saddle-bags down from the roof of the coach, making sure they landed in the dirt. He said nothing, just bent to retrieve them from the dust of San Geronimo.

FOUR

I

Malpas sat by the window and looked out on Main Street. They were already lighting the oil lamps before the saloons, the only street-lighting San Geronimo had. It was much like Coopersville, larger but not more populous and something of the Latin spirit survived here, he guessed. But probably not much.

He drew on his cigar, one of the five he'd bought in the lobby at the extortionate price of five for a dollar. If anything, it was worse than Cryper's nickel ones, but it served. He felt better. There was no getting away from it; his leg was sore now rather than painful and the ache in his stomach area was giving ground too. Only his damned thumb was the same. It didn't seem much, just one joint that had failed, but it affected more than his gunslinging. He had no real strength in his grip and it even affected his writing. When he'd scrawled his name in the hotel register the clerk had read it and called him 'Mr Mapes'. He'd laughed but not corrected him. A pseudonym? Maybe. He'd see how things were tomorrow after his visit to Squire, the fabled gunsmith.

Would it work out? But that was for tomorrow. Tonight he ought to get down from this dollar-a-night room – almost: he'd compounded at five dollars for the week – and find himself a good steak, but he knew he wouldn't. He'd finish his cigar and sleep. Eating could wait. Sleep in a soft bed couldn't. Besides, he deserved it. He'd set himself a hard task and completed it, come through and out of the Little Stony and got to San Geronimo. He'd earned a rest.

But sleep didn't come easily. He fond himself thinking of Susan Hauksbee, her finishing-school manner, her slightly *retroussé* nose, and her ridiculous affection for that ridiculous poet, Shelley. And then there was that great, florid fellow who'd swept her away.

Hell, he thought, there are plenty of pretty faces out there . . .

After an hour or so, he fell asleep.

He didn't go straight to Squire's. The hotel room had a mirror over the washstand. The shaggy, ragged and drawn creature staring out at him gave him pause. He went first to the barber's and had himself shorn and shaved. There was a bath house out back and he availed himself of its services. Then to the tailor's. He bought himself a complete new outfit, including a ready-made suit in dark, fine worsted. He felt a moment's oddness when he put it on not to affix a badge. Odd, but not unpleasant. Being one's brother's keeper was an acquired taste and one, seemingly, quite easily lost.

By then it was too near noon for Squire's so, after a brief visit to his room to transfer his cash, he found a restaurant and had a steak with good coffee and fresh-baked bread and butter. He took his time leaving, enjoying a short siesta in the shade, smoking one of the over-priced cigars. Only then did he set out to find Squire's establishment.

It wasn't hard to find. It was just off Main

Street in a big, Mexican-style adobe building with all windows set in a wall badly in need of limewashing. A sign read: J. Squire, Gunsmith.

He pushed open the door and entered the dark interior. There was nobody there in the shop proper, just a counter and racks of guns: Colts; Colt rifles with revolver cylinders set in them; Henry rifles; Winchesters. There were also sporting guns and a whole rack of Greeners of various barrel lengths and gauges. He walked over the counter, rang the bell and waited.

Squire took his timed but when he came he looked every inch the gunsmith: leather apron, strong glasses pushed up over his forehead, pale blue eyes squinting and set too near a painfully thin, aquiline nose.

'Yes?'

'I need a double-action revolver,' Malpas said, cutting to the chase.

Squire rubbed his chin. 'Do you know, nobody's ever come in and asked for that before. By dang, I doubt most of the folks hereabouts know such a thing exists.'

'But it does?' Malpas asked.

'Surely. A London gunsmith called Adams invented it and it's the future of the handgun, everywhere but here. The single-action Colt is worshipped west of the Missouri.'

'I've used one for years.'

'Oh, don't get me wrong, it's an excellent gun but it's too heavy and, forgive me, old fashioned. Colt was a genius but once he'd made his first gun he wouldn't radically improve it.' He paused. 'Excuse me for rattling on about my trade but your interest in double-action guns stimulated me, sir.' He paused again. 'Don't I know you?'

'We've never met.'

'True, but I've seen you somewhere . . . ah, I have it. In Coopersville two years ago. I was passing through and someone pointed out the famous Marshal Malpas.'

So the anonymous Mr Mapes was now lost. 'Correct.'

'I heard about the shooting and your replacement. That was not good, sir, not good at all.'

'It's done with,' Malpas said.

Squire looked at Malpas's right hand, saw the stall on the thumb and then flicked his glance to the reversed gunbelt. It was hardly necessary after that but Malpas explained anyway. 'Would a double-action gun be of help?' he concluded.

'Yes, it certainly should.'

'So may I see one?'

Squire was silent a moment. 'I'm afraid I don't stock them. No call.' He paused briefly. 'I could order you one – a few weeks?'

Malpas shook his head, was about to leave. Squire raised his hand. 'Maybe I can help, Marshal Malpas.'

'Just Malpas now.'

'Then yes, Mr Malpas. The thing is, I do have an Adams double-action revolver of sorts. It started life as a cap and ball weapon but I converted it to cartridge for my own amusement. The ammunition isn't standard—'

'How much do you have of it?'

'A hundred rounds.'

That was enough. He couldn't get much practice in but at least he'd have a weapon he could draw. 'May I see it?'

'By all means.'

The Adams revolver was a little more flashy than the Colt, had a different grip and the cylinder was unfluted. Malpas checked it was empty and hefted it, then pulled the trigger.

It was amazing to see the hammer rise and strike without the intervention of the thumb, though the gun itself did seem to move a little in his hand, but not greatly.

'You can try it downstairs in the cellar. It's where I test guns. The sound can scarcely be heard on the street.' He paused. 'But you need a new belt. I keep those downstairs too.'

'Then let's go,' Malpas said.

II

It was almost an hour later when Malpas stepped out of Squire's store into the now shadowed alley with a new gun on his hip. The new gunbelt had no loops for ammunition, just a pouch on the opposite hip. His old gun and gunbelt had gone in the way of trade. It hadn't been the hardest of bargains; he'd paid another twenty dollars for the gun and gunbelt plus a further ten for the ammunition. Even then, this gun was a stop-gap at best and he still wasn't wholly satisfied with its performance. He suspected Squire would sell his old gun at a premium too – the gun Marshal Malpas used to wipe out the Butler gang. But for all that, he could now draw and fire again. The desert had sweated the last of the fever out of him and now San Geronimo had given him power in the hand.

He found himself walking away from Main Street towards the meaner streets where the Mexicans lived, stopped and then saw the sign on the corner which read: *San Geronimo Gazette.*

Well, why not? he asked himself and walked across.

She was standing by a large table setting type by hand. To her right was the type rack and to her left a none too large and rather old-fashioned press, more suitable for printing handbills than newspapers. She was wearing a dark blue dress with a printer's apron over it. Malpas just stood and looked at her. She set down the type, turned and then smiled.

'We met on the coach, Mr . . .'

'Malpas, Jack Malpas.' Goodbye again Mr Mapes, he thought.

'Can I help you?'

'I-I came in for a paper.'

'Oh, there are several on the desk. They're all very old and out of date, I'm afraid, but just take one.' She paused. 'But you look different.'

'I shaved,' he said.

'More than that,' she said acutely, 'as if . . .' She broke off.

'I'd just walked out of the Little Stony,' Malpas said. There was no point in lying now and he didn't care to lie to her.

'That's remarkable,' she said. 'But I know your name . . . it's Marshal Malpas, isn't it?'

'It was, but I didn't know my fame had reached all the way back East.'

She smiled. 'In a way. My uncle sent me every issue and Coopersville often got a mention. But you crossed the Little Stony. Why?'

'I left off marshalling after getting wounded. I decided to come west and it was the most direct way.'

Her smile said she recognized that he wasn't telling her the whole truth but wasn't lying to her either. 'I'm sure you're being modest, Mr Malpas.'

'Call me Jack.'

'Why?'

'So I can call you Susan.'

'And why should you want to do that?'

He shrugged. 'I just do.'

'Very well then, Jack it is.'

'Do you need some help?' he asked.

'Typesetting?'

'If need be. I used to work on my father's paper back East, in an office much like this one. That was before the war, but some things you don't forget.'

'You surprise me, Jack – a marshal, a soldier, a newspaperman.'

'Not really the last. I was only part-time. I was going to be a lawyer. I joined the army instead.'

'And never went back to be either.'

'No, my father died and the paper with him. After that I couldn't afford to study law and didn't care to anyway.'

'So you became the famous Marshal Malpas.'

He didn't smile at that.

'I'm sorry, Jack, I've offended you.'

'Not at all. Do you need the help?'

'Not really. Uncle sometimes wrote the words but Mr Flynn set the type. He's off today. His rheumatism's playing him up, so I thought I'd see what I could do. He'll reset everything, believe me.' She smiled.

Malpas knew now was the time to ask her out to dinner or a drive but he didn't. Don't rush, he thought. And then there was that big, florid man. His name was Gaffney Sligo. He'd asked Squire, being careful not to refer to Susan in the question. Was there a relationship between them? There could be . . . or maybe not.

'You're staying in San Geronimo for long?'

'For a while,' he said.

'Then I'll see you again?'

'I'll call in tomorrow,' Malpas said.

'The newspaper won't be ready.'

'I'll call just in case.'

III

Outside, Malpas was both annoyed with himself and pleased at the same time. She might have accepted an invitation but then again she might not have. Somehow he knew tomorrow she would accept, he was sure of it. And this was very important to him. Maybe she knew it too. Whatever, she was not to be rushed.

He reached for a cigar, found he had none left. He could buy more at the hotel – no, he'd had enough of their over-priced rubbish. He'd find a store and buy some there. He glanced around, saw a sign painted Mexican-style on the front of an adobe building: '*Tienda*'. That meant general store.

The store was shaded inside by the buildings across but his eyes soon accustomed themselves to the gloom and he spotted the cigars on one of the shelves. There was no one about. He was on the point of rapping on the counter for attention when he heard voices coming from a backroom. It was the nature of the noise that restrained him. Not Spanish except for 'No!' much repeated and the sound of two young men laughing and talking to each other in English. Odd.

He was already on his way to check it out when he realized that this wasn't his town and he was a marshal no more, but old habits died hard and he found himself standing in the doorway of the backroom looking at two youths, one of whom was trying to kiss a young Mexican woman – the store clerk, presumably – while the other gave verbal encouragement. Kids' games? Malpas asked himself, but the one looking on had a huge Colt Dragoon pistol in his belt. Kids with guns were men.

'Stop it,' he said softly.

The words stopped the amorous kid in his tracks. He turned, fury in his face now his semi-private wooing had been interrupted. The other made no movement towards the huge Colt. Then the storm broke.

'What the hell's it to you, dude!' the first yelled, venting his fury on Malpas, standing there in the splendour of his new suit and hat.

Malpas had been too long a marshal to be overly concerned by rowdy boys, but he knew too that trouble was best avoided. 'I came in to buy some cigars. Let the young lady serve me.'

'Young lady! She's—'

'Let's not add insult to injury,' Malpas interrupted him. Then, quietly: 'It might get in the way of me buying my cigars and I wouldn't recommend that at all.'

The other rowdy's hand had been moving towards the Colt. Hearing the steel in Malpas's voice, it veered away.

Malpas looked them over as the episode briefly became a tableau vivant – a pair of 17-year-olds in rather worn shirts and trousers, both hatless. Even their boots looked home-made. Suddenly he wearied of it all, flicked back his coat to reveal the gun and let his hand poise over it. 'Get out now,' he said, not so softly as before and with all the firmness of authority.

They obeyed, sidling past him into the body of the shop. At the door the amorous one turned back briefly but the other stayed him. Then they both left.

'Oh, *señor*...' and the girl launched into a fusillade of fast Spanish far beyond his basic conversational skills, but he still understood her perfectly.

'*No es nada, señorita,*' he essayed then switched to English. 'Would you sell me some cigars? That's what I came in for: cigars.'

And suddenly she was laughing. Tears would follow, he knew, but he hoped to be out the shop before then.

'The cigars,' he said, 'I'll take ten of them.'

He hadn't expected a confrontation in the street but he hadn't discounted one either, so he wasn't too surprised to see the amorous one of the pair waiting for him in Main Street, the big Colt stuck in his belt now. He didn't trouble to look for the other one. They'd only the one gun between them.

'I'm calling you out, dude,' the young man screamed out in his fury.

Malpas said nothing. It was past the time for words. He again flicked back his coat from his gun, checked the distance between them, forty yards, noting how empty Main Street was. That was usual but it didn't mean nobody was watching. People were – from the windows and doorways, and he wasn't wearing a marshal's badge anymore. The kid had to draw first. He started walking towards him. He drew at twenty yards, pulling the big gun out of his belt with some speed. The pair of them had obviously been practising. But so had Malpas, and for longer. He drew too and got off the first shot, hitting the kid in the shoulder even as he brought the Colt up to firing position. The bullet went wild, then the gun fell from his hand and he fell on his knees in the dirt.

It was only then the street came to life. Malpas ignored everything but the Colt which he went over to and collected. He didn't want the partner to have a chance at a second go.

'I'll take charge of that,' said the man with a marshal's badge pinned to his chest who came running up. Then: 'Jack!'

'Sam,' Malpas said, acknowledging Sam Crystalman. They'd been deputies together in Santa Fe once.

'I heard you were out of it. Glad to see you're not. What's it all about?'

Malpas told him.

'So you want him charged?'

Malpas shook his head. 'He called me out fair and square. Besides, he's got the bullet in him. As for the girl . . .'

'She'll be happy leaving it as it is,' Sam Crystalman said. He unloaded the Colt – it had been converted to cartridge – and then tossed the empty weapon towards the kid who was still on his knees. 'I want you out of San Geronimo now. Your pal can take you. And the next time I see you in this town, I'll kill you myself. Stick to Polvertown and your own kind.' Then he turned back to Malpas. 'Come on, I'll buy you a drink. That was a damn fine shot.'

Malpas didn't argue though he knew it wasn't. He was too old a hand to play games with guns. He'd aimed for the heart.

IV

Night was falling on San Geronimo. The saloon keepers were coming out and turning

66

off the lamps now their trade had departed. San Geronimo wasn't a town with night-lighting that lasted, like Santa Fe or New York. Oil cost money and the lamps were private property.

Malpas lit a cigar as he stood by the window watching the town fade into dimness, reflecting upon the events of the day. Particularly one event, and not the shooting either. Marshal Crystalman had told him about Polvertown and Josiah Polver in the bar – the true tale, he'd said – of how after the Mexican-American war when the US government had guaranteed to uphold Spanish land grants, Josiah Polver had got around that by kidnapping the members of the Santiago clan left in the US and only despatching them back to Mexico when José Santiago, who virtually ruled the northern part of the state of Chihuahua, ceded his US lands to him, since which time the local border had been a difficult place indeed.

In fact, Polver had done himself no favours for he was a better kidnapper than a rancher and over the years he'd had to sell off the best bits to pay his taxes, keeping only the land around the old northern hacienda, now called

Polvertown, and just surviving by rustling from his northern neighbours. For all that, he'd quite a clan down there of sons, relatives, adopted drifters and the Mexican servants who stayed. Sam Crystalman hated the lot of them.

Interesting, Malpas thought, but so what? He recalled Crystalman from his Santa Fe days. He was quiet tempered but nervous minded, passing honest but a little on the stupid side. Why should he care what he thought?

Except he'd mentioned Susan Hauksbee in passing. 'You came in on the stage with her, didn't you?'

Malpas had nodded, adding, 'I saw her at the newspaper office today.'

Sam Crystalman had shrugged. 'That's always losing money. Tom Hauksbee kept it as a hobby. She'll have better things on her mind when she's married.'

'Who to?'

'I hear tell there's some arrangement with Gaffney Sligo. He owns the Double X ranch, right next to the Hauksbee spread.'

He'd said nothing to that; besides, it had been time for Crystalman to make his rounds. Malpas hadn't come straight up to his room then but forced himself to have dinner and play a hand or two at cards, winning twenty dollars to boot, but his heart hadn't been in it. So it was Gaffney Sligo, the big florid man he'd seen with her at the stage. . . .

He'd said he'd call on her tomorrow but there seemed no point to that any longer. On impulse, he opened the window and tossed the cigar butt out, a brief falling star before it was lost in the dust of Main Street.

V

Susan Hauksbee urged on the horse pulling her buggy. The note had said there was an emergency at the ranch and she should get there immediately, though not what it was. She'd found it pushed under her door and it wasn't even signed but she knew Ken Rivers, the foreman, was no penman. She'd even been tempted to ignore it, guessing it would turn out to be nothing much, but it was the family ranch and she had a duty to it.

She found herself remembering making this same journey as a girl, beside her father, and with him singing in his fine baritone:

The trees shade the river,
The clouds hide the land . . .

A tear came to her eye but she didn't let
herself go further. He'd been dead these seven
years. His brother, uncle Tom, had been dead
just six weeks and she'd no tears for him
though she'd loved him well enough, but the
tears had been shed back East. Leave them
there; they served no purpose.

She glanced off the trail at the empty range
around her. The ranch made her an heiress
but scarcely a rich one. What savings the family
once had had all been spent on the paper and
her fancy education, and after land taxes and
wages they were just breaking even. Yes, she'd
be sure to tell Jack Malpas that, smiling to
herself as she thought of him.

She hadn't known of the gunfight until it
was over and had almost rushed out to see
him, but stopped herself in time. He wasn't a
man to be pushed. There was a reticence
about him that was unusual in a man who'd
come through the Little Stony and faced a
gang of robbers alone and triumphed. All the
same, she'd left a note for him at the office,
not too inviting but not discouraging either. It

was odd how you could become so fond of someone you'd only seen twice, but she had. Even on the coach she'd half known it. If that fool Sligo hadn't pounced on her just after she'd arrived. . . .

She smiled. He'd virtually proposed there and then, on the street, talking of an 'arrangement' with her uncle. As if she could be bartered by men in this day and age! It had been all she could manage to be coldly polite.

It was then she noticed the two riders on the skyline, saw them coming towards her. They'd be from the ranch, she thought, coming out to escort her in and she didn't slow the buggy down at all.

FIVE

I

Events had moved quickly. When Malpas had finally gone to the newspaper office, if only to keep his word – he was a stickler for that, having discovered long since that honesty was not simply the best but by far the easiest policy – he'd had no more than a minute or so to digest the contents of her note before he heard that Gaffney Sligo had come to town in force, along with Ken Rivers, the Hauksbee foreman, bringing the news that Susan's buggy had been found abandoned on the Polvertown trail.

A public meeting had been called, supposedly presided over by the mayor, Mr Thorogood

– it turned out he was neither preacher nor undertaker, just another saloon keeper – but in reality controlled by Gaffney Sligo himself. It was held in the church – the court and council chamber were equally too small for a town meeting – and now Sligo stood before the altar table like the wrath of God, his face a fiery red and his voice booming.

Malpas was angry himself, angrier than he had ever been before in his life. The note had seemingly said little, just that she would be back that evening, but that was in itself a great deal. Susan wasn't a girl to write notes like that to another man if she were engaged in any way to Gaffney Sligo. For a couple of minutes it had buoyed his spirits, then the terrible news.

'It could all be quite innocent,' said an incautious man in the body of the church.

'Don't be a damned fool, Fairclough! It all fits. Yesterday two rapists from Polvertown were sent scuttling back to their rats' nest by Marshal Malpas – our thanks to him – and today Susan Hauksbee is kidnapped.' He paused, then: 'Excuse me if I'm too harsh, but I have a special feeling for my old friend's daughter. But that aside, consider the evidence. She received a note saying there was

an emergency at the Hauksbee spread. There
wasn't, as Ken Rivers here can confirm. But we
know of the note because she told Bill Galley
at the livery. Is there anybody here who doubts
his word?'

No one spoke.

'Next, the buggy was spotted on the
Polvertown trail by my riders. That was pure
chance as it's on the very edge of my property,
but there'd been steers lost and my riders were
investigating and, finding it, came to me. I
came to town, spoke to Billy Galley.' He
paused again.

'You might think it's a bit obvious but the
only reason the horse hadn't trotted back on
its own was because it was plumb tuckered out.
Another hour and it would have bethought
itself of the pleasant stall and the oats waiting
for it at the livery, and come back on its own. If
that had happened we'd never have known
where she was. We've been very lucky.

'But the real clincher is that a Polver was
shot yesterday. Rightfully. But you all know
Josiah Polver. You all know how he got his
ranch in the first place. Now that he's on the
verge of losing it for unpaid taxes – we've all
had cattle rustled or just plain gone missing –

what's more likely than he's come up with the same idea again?

'I reckon there's no doubt about where Susan is being held and no doubt either as to what red-blooded, freeborn Americans should do about it. I call upon Marshal Crystalman to organize a posse to bring back Susan Hauksbee and root out the thieves, murderers and rapists of Polvertown!'

Malpas, who had kept to the back, walked out of the church. He knew what was coming next. Marshal Crystalman would protest he had no authority beyond city limits and then be empowered by a vote of all present – a dubious legal device but it would be a rare judge who questioned it later in a nation founded on the concept of 'We, the people'. And Crystalman wouldn't command much anyway. Gaffney Sligo would, both his own men and the Hauksbee cowboys and any other cowboys present.

So be it. Malpas was content. Gaffney Sligo had been crude but convincing. He'd go along but to do that he needed more than just a sidearm.

Squire was in his shop, as he'd guessed. Gunsmiths rarely pushed themselves forward when weapons were to be used.

'A Winchester?'

Malpas shook his head. 'Never used one, always a Henry repeater. But there'll be plenty of riflemen going along. I'll take a sawn-off Greener if you have one.'

Squire scratched his chin, disappeared into the back of his shop, then reappeared with a curious weapon, a Mexican-style pistola, a shotgun cut down to the size of a horse pistol but a touch on the bulky side.

'Mexican work,' Malpas said dismissively.

'Some of it's bad,' Squire agreed, 'but the best is unsurpassed. This isn't quite that but it might be useful. The top two barrels work just like a shotgun. The third barrel is buried under them in the stock itself. Do this—' and he touched what looked like part of the ornamentation and a trigger sprang out below just ahead of the regular ones. 'Pull it and a .32 bullet is fired, low power but cut cruciform. It'll take down anything within ten feet of you. The very devil to reload but . . .'

'OK,' Malpas said. 'How much—'

'You're going out looking for Miss Hauksbee, aren't you?'

'Yes.'

'You'll need a horse. Take mine. You can go as my surrogate. It's the sorrel in the last stall on the left in the livery. All I ask is that you bring Susan Hauksbee back.'

'She'll be found and brought back,' Malpas said softly. 'Count on that.'

II

They'd ridden hard and were only seven miles from Polvertown when night fell. Sligo wanted to continue. A night attack would be devastating, he said.

'No,' Malpas said, as they stood by their horses in conclave.

'Look here,' Gaffney Sligo said, 'maybe you're hell on wheels in Texas, but this ain't Texas. You started this thing by shooting one of Polver's bastards. I've been polite to you so far—'

'And you'll continue to be,' Malpas said in a voice that brooked no disagreement. He let the silence persist for a moment, then continued, 'I'm probably saving your life. You're right, a night attack can be devastating but you need disciplined men—'

'My men are that.'

'They're cowboys. They've not been trained for war and taking any town is war. Go in at first light when you can see who you're shooting at. You still have the element of surprise and they're still groggy from sleep. It'll work.'

'You were a soldier, sir?' asked one of the ranch owners with Southern politeness.

'Yes, sir. I was a captain in the cavalry.'

And that settled it. Malpas guessed he'd converted even Sligo, though the latter didn't admit it. Malpas didn't press him. He knew it was better to have one bad leader rather than two good ones. When he'd commanded a company he would not have appreciated the newest recruit trying to take over.

Eventually a compromise was reached. As the main street in Polvertown ran north-south and they'd be approaching by curving round at the close, it was possible Polver might flee with his prisoner to the north, therefore the force would be split, the southern force under Sligo and the northern one under Crystalman. So Malpas found himself under Sam Crystalman's command.

'It's for the best,' the town marshal said as they mounted up. 'Hell, you can be my second-in-command.'

'Why not?' Malpas said, knowing his advice had saved lives. Besides, he would be glad to get away from Gaffney Sligo. The man rubbed him the wrong way and Malpas had been in a cold, killing rage ever since he'd learnt Susan had been kidnapped.

'Let's ride,' Crystalman said, and the tiny company rode slowly off into the dark. They'd given Crystalman just four riflemen, if you counted Winchesters as rifles, which Malpas didn't. They weren't even the equivalent of military carbines, which meant shortened rifles. Winchesters only fired a handgun bullet from a longish barrel, albeit a lot of them and quickly. But it didn't matter. It was Gaffney Sligo who'd be leading the main assault force on Polvertown.

Crystalman didn't know the way. There was no reason why he should. He was a town marshal, not a county sheriff, and Malpas guessed he rarely ventured beyond the triangle formed by the nearest saloon, his jailhouse and his hotel room. None of the cowboys were Sligo men, on whose land this bordered, so they were no better informed. Thus, a little sooner than he'd anticipated, the second-in-command took over.

'There's the pole star, see,' he said, pointing. 'Due north. We go in the opposite direction for seven miles and we're there.'

Crystalman was pleased. He could see no further problems. Malpas wasn't so sure. Sligo did know this land and he'd chosen this way for them.

It didn't take long to find out why. Malpas had thought the horizon had seemed odd, high and close, and they soon found out the reason: the land was no longer flat but undulating, made up of a series of roughly east to west ridges, not too high but broad, waves in a frozen sea. Despite themselves it was hard to keep exactly due south as they negotiated the way to the next undulation.

It tired the already well-ridden horses too. Malpas stopped them atop a ridge. 'We'd better get off and walk.'

'What?' asked Crystalman.

'The horses are tired out,' Malpas said. 'They need rest and food. We can't give them either so we do the next best thing: we take ourselves off their backs and spare them the weight, twenty minutes or so every

80

hour. That's how the cavalry avoid becoming infantry.'

One of the cowboys volunteered that he'd seen soldiers doing that near Fort Gellhorn and Crystalman gave in with moderately bad grace.

'I suppose you know what you're talking about.'

'Most of the time,' Malpas said bitterly. The whole of his anger and fury came out in those few words and surprised even him, but at least he had no more complaints.

Negotiating the ridges seemed to take forever – up and down, sometimes walking, sometimes riding, and the night seemingly lasting forever. But it didn't. The sky lightened a little and Malpas realized they'd not make Polvertown by dawn, never mind by what Sligo would interpret as first light. They were walking at the time. He stopped them. 'Let's mount up and ride.'

He'd hoped the next ridge would be the last one. It wasn't and already they could see the first glimmerings of the rising sun on their left. They could also see now how deep the riverless valleys were. If they'd ridden continuously they'd have exhausted their horses an hour back.

Crack! There was no mistaking the sound of a gunshot and many, many more followed in quick succession. A mile off, Malpas guessed, maybe a mile and a quarter. He said nothing, just touched spurs lightly to the flanks of the sorrel and was away, certain the little troop would follow him.

III

There were six of them, coming north out of Polvertown. They saw them on the skyline, on the ridge itself, riding hard four hundred yards ahead of them. They were all men, and young men at that, so Sligo had been successful in Polvertown itself. Certainly, Susan was not amongst them.

'Dismount,' Malpas commanded. They did so, even Crystalman. 'Use your Winchesters,' he said. 'Wait until they're around a hundred and fifty yards off and then let them have it. The marshal and I will hold the horses and join in with our handguns if they get close.'

They did as ordered, Crystalman too, and the cowboys were very good shots indeed. The

Polvertown boys were game, coming down the slope at the gallop, closing the distance instead of trying to make it a firefight with long arms as they should have. But three of them were down at a hundred yards, two more at fifty and only one got near enough to fire his weapon – a Navy Colt. He missed. Crystalman killed him with his Colt, emptying it into him while still holding the reins of three horses with his left hand.

Malpas told them to reload, waited until they had, and he and Sam Crystalman returned their horses to them. He mounted up and rode over to the first of the Polvertown men. It was the boy who'd called him out, his shoulder bound up in a dirty dressing, lying dead beside his horse.

The rest were of much the same age, except for one man in his thirties who'd been shot in the belly. One of the cowboys finished him off with his Winchester, just as they shot the wounded horses. Malpas said nothing. That was how war was fought whatever it said in the manuals, and he needed to get to Polvertown fast. Besides, he thought a little grimly, it was up to Crystalman. He was the nominal commander.

He also saw why they'd charged. Not one of them had a long weapon, just Colts and mostly cap and ball ones at that. A charge had been their only chance.

It proved to be the last ridge. Below they saw Polvertown spread out before them in the early morning light. The original hacienda buildings could be seen in its centre, run down now, and all around were shacks and lean-to's – a town of hovels.

There was still some residual shooting but Malpas had no doubt Gaffney Sligo had taken the town. The kid hadn't run from victory and whatever else he might have been, he hadn't been a coward.

With their destination in sight Crystalman suddenly took over, charging to the front and shouting, 'Follow me!'

Malpas suppressed a smile and did just that.

No way had Polvertown been expecting an attack. The cowboys had ridden in and found no real opposition, which hadn't stopped them from killing the men. There were corpses scattered throughout the rough, unpaved streets, some with ancient hand-weapons or shotguns still by them, some without. And an old man hung from the watch-tower of the hacienda, still in his nightshirt, his scrawny legs visible. He'd also been shot many times but *post mortem*. His neck was broken. It was virtually impossible to break the neck of a corpse by hanging.

It was Josian Polver, he was certain, and Crystalman confirmed it.

'Hell,' the marshal said, 'they've ripped the guts out of the place!'

Malpas said nothing more. It was indisputable. And as they rode on, at a statelier pace now, they saw groups of women milling about, still in their shifts, and weeping.

'She's not here,' Gaffney Sligo said. 'I've torn the town apart looking for her.'

'Yeah,' said one of his cowboys unprompted, 'we done that for sure!'

'They didn't bring her here, obviously,' Sligo said. 'My best guess is that she'll be in a lineshack somewhere east of here. But be sure of one thing, we'll find her.'

He sounded sincere, Malpas thought, but with some people that was just a knack. And one Sligo possessed in full measure, Malpas was sure. But he believed him that Susan had never been here, in Polvertown. In fact, he was morally certain of it.

'What now?' Crystalman asked.

'We burn the place,' Sligo said, smiling openly.

That was too much even for Marshal Sam Crystalman. 'Hell, Gaffney, what about the women and kids?'

'We won't harm them. They can take their clothes and food and whatever they can carry and leave, but leave they will. Polvertown's finished for good.'

'I ain't sure I can go along with that,' Crystalman said. 'When all's said and done this is my posse and—'

'This isn't San Geronimo, Sam,' Sligo said. 'I seem to recall at the town meeting you telling us all that it wasn't in your bailiwick and I reckon you were right then. Leave it in the hands of me and my boys. We know what we're about.'

Crystalman fell silent. It was true he'd said that. It was also true that half the men here were cowboys who worked for Sligo and the vast majority of the remainder were cowboys too, men who would have no time at all for rustlers or their families.

'Have you anything to say, Mr Malpas?' Sligo asked, looking at him.

'You've said it all,' Malpas said.

SIX

I

Squire opened the door and looked question-ingly at Malpas, but it was the latter who asked the question.

'Why have you closed early?'

'Who's about to buy anything today?' Squire said. 'Come in and tell me everything.'

Malpas did, not in the shop but in a small apartment over it, well furnished in Mexican style and spotlessly clean.

'So you had no opportunity to use the pistols,' Squire said when Malpas had finished.

'I shot no one,' Malpas said, 'and I'm glad of it.' He paused. 'By the way, your sorrel's back in the livery, rather worse for wear but uninjured.'

'Good,' Squire said. 'Would you like another bourbon? No, then tell me why you've come here. Not simply to inform me about my horse, I think.'

'I came because it seemed to me you care about Susan Hauksbee.'

'Just because I lent you a horse?'

'You used the word "surrogate" too,' Malpas said. 'A man employed to do *your* duty.'

Squire leaned back in his chair, then looked across at Malpas. 'You're a remarkable man, Mr Malpas. You're quite right, of course. I was a friend of her father, Stewart Hauksbee. A real friend. In those days this was a newly conquered territory and we stuck together. More than that, my late wife was not blessed with children and when Susan's mother died she . . . But enough of my life. As you guessed, I've very fond of her.'

'I still intend to get her back.'

'If she's in a lineshack, Sligo will—'

'No, Sligo's the one who arranged the kidnapping.'

Squire was silent a moment. 'He's capable of most things. I know that full well, but—'

'Why should he do it? Because she wouldn't marry him.' Malpas took the note out of his pocket, handed it to Squire. 'Would Susan have written that to me if she were engaged to him?'

Squire read it. 'It's arguable, but knowing Susan, no. Not that the note itself says much at all.'

'It's enough that she sent it to me.'

'Does Sligo know about this?' He handed back the note.

'No.'

'Then don't let him.' He paused, sighed. 'It might just make sense. With her gone, the Hauksbee ranch would be in limbo. He could encroach on its range without any significant penalty. Eventually he might even be able to buy it cheap. Better to get it by marriage but I agree with you, that wasn't on the cards. But where is she? Dead and buried?'

'No, no, I've seen the man in action. He's ruthless but not stupid. And ask yourself another question, who else gains from this affair?'

'I don't follow.'

'There's much more to it than just the Hauksbee range. Ask yourself about the reason for attacking Polvertown. Who most wanted to see Polver hanged in his nightshirt?'

'José Santiago!'

'Now you see why I came to you. I need information about the Santiago clan. I'm counting on you.'

Squire raised a hand. 'There's someone who knows the Santiagos far better than I do.'

'Someone we can trust?'

Squire nodded. 'Stay here, I might be minutes, I might be hours, but you'll get the man you need. In the meantime, *mi casa es su casa.*' And with that, he left.

Taking him at his word, Malpas helped himself to another bourbon and a cigar from the box on the table. It wasn't of the nickel variety either, but he'd scarcely finished smoking it before Seuire returned with Mr Flynn from the newspaper.

'I've told him everything you told me,' Squire said, 'so ask away.'

'I need more than newspaper gossip,' Malpas said sceptically.

'And you shall have it,' Flynn said, sitting down, refusing a bourbon with a gesture of his hand. 'But it might be useful if I were to tell you about myself. . . .'

II

'When I gave you the note in the newspaper office,' Flynn said, 'you barely noticed me. An odd-looking Irishman you thought, but then there are many odd-looking people in the world. But not so odd if you had known my name, my full name, which is Juan Flynn y Mendoza.

'The original Flynn left Ireland two centuries ago, I believe, but we were proud of the name. My father worked for the Santiagos. We lived in the hacienda and he was killed, defending them when Josiah Polver kidnapped the junior branch of the family who lived there.

'At the time, I was in Chihuahua City studying to be an *abogado* – an advocate, a lawyer. I was to work for the Santiagos in that profession. But that ended. My fees were no longer paid, I was no longer welcome. You may find that strange, but then you do not understand the Santiagos.

'The first Santiago came with Cortes. He was a conquistador for all that he had been just a peasant in Extramadura, and he founded a line. His descendants became barons, counts, marquesses, but the titles were unimportant. The Santiagos were conquistadors. They had more power over their lands and people than even a Spanish Grandee of the first class enjoyed in Spain, and for all the talk of democracy in Mexico City, in Chihuahua the demos – the people – were nothing and José de Santiago everything. . . .

'I could have gone south to Mexico City where half-trained lawyers starved or I could come home; a home where the Americans now rule. As I already spoke English – and wasn't my name Flynn? – the choice was easy.

'And I was very lucky. I met Stewart Hauksbee and became his clerk, then his lawyer. Oh, not formally. Even now I am a mere notary public, but in effect I was the Hauksbee lawyer. I could speak both languages and soon enough I knew both codes of law. I did much to build up the Hauksbee ranch; enough so that when my son was born, Stewart Hauksbee gave me a thousand acres to build up a horse ranch. It's to the west of town and I still own it, though my son runs it now, of course.

'When Stewart died Tom became Susan's guardian. He was more interested in the newspaper than anything. Incidentally, we have never made a profit yet. But I helped in that, too, though he preferred a proper American lawyer. His neighbour probably suggested that. Tom was always very much under Gaffney Sligo's thumb.

'But things change and one put up with them. The horse ranch was flourishing, as does my son and his family. Why should I complain? Who would care if I did? And then Susan was coming home. Things might change again.

'They did, horribly. Foolishly, I believed it was all Polver's work until Squire here came to me, told me what you thought.

'You are a clever man, Marshal Malpas, but Susan told me that. She was much taken with you, I could see. I'll be honest, I disapproved. But I think I was wrong. You are taken with her, too. Sometimes it happens so. And so I will answer your questions, but first let me get myself a bourbon.'

But it was Squire who got him his bourbon, a full glass of it which he downed as if it were sarsaparilla. And it was Squire, too, who asked the first question.

'Then you're sure it was Sligo who kidnapped her?'

'Weren't you listening?' Flynn asked, somewhat irritably. 'Sligo will have played his part, but the men who took her would have been Santiago men. Sligo asked her to marry him virtually as soon as she stepped off the coach, but that was a last ditch attempt to avoid all this. The planning must have been done long before. Perhaps it was as well for Sligo he was refused. José is an unforgiving man.'

'And one with a hold over Gaffney Sligo?' Malpas said.

'Probably gambling debts,' Flynn agreed. 'I'd guess he's collected up all his markers. José de Santiago is a clever man, and he chose his pawn carefully. With Susan gone, Gaffney Sligo has San Geronimo and its environs in his pocket, and Santiago has him in his pocket.'

'No doubt,' Malpas said, 'but it doesn't help me. I need to know just where she is.'

'Somewhere in the great state of Chihuahua.'

'That narrows it down,' Squire said ironically.

'True, and we can narrow it down further,' Flynn went on. 'As I said, it's my guess Santiago sent men across the border to kidnap a US citizen. Were that to become common knowledge it would be very dangerous even for him, especially with Mexico City. He can kill a thousand Mexicans with impunity but US citizens are another matter, and violating the border to do it more so. She must still be alive so she can be returned if need be, and because of that she cannot be on any Santiago property.'

'Somewhere near the border, but not too near,' Malpas put in. 'Somewhere defensible, but not too obviously so. And on the property of someone ostensibly at odds with the Santiagos.'

'Pablo Italico!' Squire interjected.

Malpas looked to Flynn. 'Who's he talking about?'

'The Santiagos have been at odds with Italicos for generations. The Italicos lost much of their lands to the United States in the war. They have become weak. José could destroy them, but they are conquistadors too so he will not. The people must never see a conquistador fall. It might give them ideas.'

'But Santiago will have his way eventually,' Malpas said.

'Oh, yes. An Italico heir will marry a

Santiago and the Italicos will become a junior branch of the family.'

'But if a favour were done, the match could involve a higher grade Santiago.'

Flynn looked at Malpas intently. 'You know Mexico well.'

'No,' Malpas said. 'I learned a bit of Spanish – not hard if you know Latin – but in my youth I studied history. That's how things have always been done.' He paused. 'So Pablo Italico it is?'

'Yes,' Flynn said. 'But she won't be at the main hacienda. Pablo, too, will exercise care.' He paused, then said, 'I need a map, an old one.'

Squire got to his feet. 'I sell maps too,' he said. 'But the trade in guns is better.'

There was only one place that fitted, a manorial farm fifteen miles west and seventeen miles south of the border. It was called Casa del Norte.

'How many men there?' Malpas asked.

'I don't know,' Flynn said. 'There'll be peons in the shacks around the hacienda proper but they won't be armed. Certainly not many beside Pablo himself, maybe just the two who brought her there. The fewer in on the secret the better. Beyond that, I can't say.'

That made sense, Malpas thought. It all did, a horrible kind of sense. Crime usually did. This Santiago was cleverer than most criminals but his subtlety merely disguised a crude revenge.

'We'll need help,' Squire said. 'I'll see Thorogood and Cystalman—'

'No,' Malpas said.

'But—'

'You're going to invade Mexico with a posse? On what evidence?'

'But you've just heard it.'

'I've heard some old tales, added in a few speculations of my own, but nothing more than that. Sligo would deny everything and Crystalmen would back him. So would every other man of substance hereabouts. They've just sacked and burnt Polvertown and hung the man who did the crime. Do you think they're going to admit they were wrong?'

Squire shook his head in silence.

Malpas looked to Flynn. 'I'll need two horses, saddled, and with full canteens. I'll also need a letter in Spanish with a certain signature. Can you oblige me?'

'It's not a signature a man forgets,' Flynn

said. 'Write what you want. I'll turn it into Spanish. The horses will be outside town at dawn. And God help you.'

'One more thing,' Malpas asked. 'What would happen to Susan if . . .' He let the sentence hang in the air.

'Not death,' Flynn said. 'The Santiago hostages were all returned alive. But the women had been raped. . . .' He broke off.

Malpas didn't press him. He understood full well. Santiago would want his full and complete revenge. Susan would be sold to some brothel owner, beaten into submission and dishonour.

He saw both of them looking away from him and knew why. There was death in his expression, maybe his own too, but not his alone.

Not by a long way.

III

It was a different Flynn who met him outside town just after dawn, a tall man of about thirty on a tall horse with the reins of two spare horses, both sorrels, in his hands. The son, obviously.

'I'm Anders Flynn. Pa told me everything. If you need help, I'll come with you.'

'Thanks but no,' Malpas said, looking over the horses. They were excellent specimens. 'It's a job for a troop of cavalry or just one man. Two would just make it more dangerous.'

Anders Flynn didn't argue. 'You also need this.' He handed Malpas a sheet of paper folded like an envelope and sealed. 'He said it's better not to break the seal. The text is just what you wrote but it's now in Spanish over the signature you asked for.'

'How did he manage the seal?' Malpas asked.

'From something left to him by my grandpa. Pa took it off that with a hot knife, washed it in soap and water. It looks real fresh.'

It did. 'He got the signature from the same letter?'

'Yes, sir.'

'I'm obliged to him – please tell him that.'

'He'd've come himself but he was plumb tuckered out. I insisted. If there's anything more I can do. . . .'

'You've already done it,' Malpas said. He slipped the letter into his pocket, checked his guns – just the Adams revolver and the pistola, the latter now in a holster fastened to his belt that Squire had provided. Squire had also insisted he take the bed last night but despite being up the night before he hadn't slept much, three hours at best. It didn't matter. He'd slept less, much less than that in the war and this too was war of a sort.

He crossed the border an hour later. There was nothing to see, just scrub, and only the map itself insisted there was a border at all.

For all he had started out early, Malpas was in no hurry to get to Casa del Norte. He needed to scout the land on the way and arriving at the end of siesta would be about right. He would have preferred to arrive just before dark, to avoid any pursuit on leaving, but that would have looked suspicious. And if everything worked out as planned, it should be easy. Santiago demanded obedience. Demand it in his name with a letter over his signature and it was yours too.

Maybe.

And maybe not. Was he even sure Susan was being held in Casa del Norte? Or that all the talk of last night hadn't been so much moonshine?

He went over it in his mind as he rode,

taking it apart item by item. Santiago wanted revenge on Polver. Polver was dead, hanged. That had all started with a kidnapping, so then had this. It also suited Santiago's cat's-paw, Gaffney Sligo, over whom he had some sort of hold. In effect, it would give Santiago control at a distance of all the land around San Geronimo, land which had once been his.

He found he didn't doubt any of that. It was beyond resonable doubt. The real question was whether Susan Hauksbee was being held against her will in Casa del Norte. There was more supposition there, that was merely right on the balance of probabilities, but he felt in his bones that she was. It made sense.

After an hour's riding, he changed horses. He needed to keep them both as fresh as possible. He nooned about five miles from Casa del Norte, wetting the horses' noses from a canteen and letting them graze on the scant grass. He dined on the bread he found in the saddle-bags, then smoked a cigar. The waiting was harder than he'd anticipated; he found he was anxious to be going, to bring things to a conclusion.

It might be his conclusion, he thought. Maybe a very unpleasant one. This was Mexico and they did things very differently here. So be it. He had to die sometime, somewhere, and he could think of no better cause.

He made himself light a second cigar but it didn't relax him one bit. All he could think of was that this was very open country, no cover at all to speak of. If it came to a fight the odds would be fantastically against him.

IV

It was morning. The light from the high, barred window awakened her from her uneasy sleep on the narrow bed and she sat up, clutching the blankets about her. Another day.

Soon the woman would bring her food and coffee and refuse to answer her questions again. Susan had almost forgotten she spoke Spanish; there had been no call for it back East, but the language of her childhood nurse – her wet nurse to begin with – had come back to her almost automatically.

It had done her no good. Even yesterday when they'd let her spend the afternoon out of this cell in the other room with the women, no one would tell her where she was or who held her. They'd chatted about their men and other women's children but whenever she asked direct questions, they looked away. They were afraid. And when they'd brought her back, she'd seen something like pity in their eyes.

Susan shivered. If only someone would come . . . but that was foolishness. If she didn't know where she was, or why she was here, how could anyone else? She'd fantasised about Jack Malpas coming, but who was he to her? No one was coming. As far as San Geronimo was concerned, the range had simply swallowed her up.

She shuddered a little at the thought, but there might well be worse things. Those flashes of pity in dark eyes troubled her. A forced marriage? Worse?

It would probably be even worse than that. . . .

Then the bolt was drawn back, the door opened and the woman with the tray entered.

'*Señorita,*' she said, and set it down on the floor, not meeting her eyes. Then she was gone and the door bolted behind her.

Susan made no move to get up and go for the food, tortillas, goat's cheese and a huge cup of steaming hot coffee. No knife or fork but there never was. For the moment they wanted her alive and didn't care to trust her with a knife.

And the awful thought came to her that they were right. She would not submit to living as a degraded slave. It was a terrible thought but she confronted it, accepted it. Maybe it wouldn't come to that but if it did, she'd find a way.

After a while the smell of coffee tempted her from the bed and she ate and drank. Then she sat there, on the narrow bed, beyond tears.

SEVEN

I

The hacienda Casa del Norte had been built in the centre of a slight declivity so that Malpas came upon it suddenly: the flat land became a ridge looking down on it – a walled hacienda of some age surrounded by hovels. Much like Polvertown, he thought, though the hovels here were decently limed and more picturesque.

There were corrals to the south of the *ad hoc* town but beyond them, nothing, just scrub-land as far as the eye could see.

He considered the hacienda itself. It was gated at the north and south, the eastern wall being part of the house, the western side part of the stables. It was probably two centuries old and in those two centuries nothing had happened to it except for the inevitable lime-washes.

And then Susan Hauksbee had been brought here. He felt the anger rise in his throat, controlled it. Everything depended on him not being angry, just a man doing a job, nothing more.

He lit a cigar, changed horses and started slowly down the slope towards Casa del Norte.

Riding through the streets between the shacks, he scarcely saw anyone, just a naked child in a doorway, a flash of eyes behind a glassless window, nothing else. Strangers here were bad news and, anyway, nothing for a peon to concern himself with. But that was to the good for once: one less threat.

No one stopped him at the southern gate and he rode through. There was a hitching rail just before the main door and he tied both horses there, walked slowly up to the door itself and rapped on it. It was made of oak, certainly not local, and was full of iron studs. A coat of arms had been carved into its centre but it was now worn down and obscured by much polishing.

After a few seconds waiting, a man opened the door to him. He was no peon: he was wearing a revolver slung low on his thigh and there was more than a touch of coldness in his eyes.

'I'm here to see Don Pablo de Italico,' Malpas said, then repeated it in his bad Spanish.

The man smiled, gestured for him to enter. Malpas did so, found himself in a small vestibule from which he was led into a large room dominated by the massive oak table in its centre. But this was not the master's table, he guessed; it was old, crudely made and polished only by use. Standing to one side of it was another man, wearing two guns, both slung low and with a crossbelt of pouches over his left shoulder. He smiled; gold glinted in the dim light.

'*Señor*, I am Don Pablo's tophand – that is how you say it?'

'It is,' Malpas said.

'And you have come from the north to see him, you say?'

'I have.' He paused, raised his hand to his jacket. '*Con permiso?*'

'Of course.'

Malpas took out the letter. 'For Don Pablo. I am instructed to put it into his hand and his alone.'

The two-gun man scratched his chin, then said, 'I see it, no?'

Malpas walked around the table and stood before him, showed it to him but did not put it in the outstretched hand.

He wasn't asked to do so. The seal had been recognized. Malpas guessed that these were not Italico men but Santiago's own.

'If the *señor* will wait here,' the man with two guns said and left.

Malpas put the letter away, considered sitting but the only seats were benches pushed under the table itself and he decided against it.

He noticed the first man was watching him closely, but that his hand was nowhere near his gun. Both these men would be fast draws, Malpas guessed, quick as rattlers but without their innate charm. In fact, the chances were that this pair had kidnapped Susan.

'You speak English?' he asked the remaining man.

'He scarcely speaks Spanish,' said the two-gun man coming back into the room. They

109

both laughed, shrilly and without humour.

'Don Pablo de Italico will see you, *señor*, but . . .' He gestured towards the gun Malpas wore.

Carefully, Malpas drew the pistola, broke it open and extracted the two cartridges, placing them on the table. He then put the pistola back in its holster. '*Era de mi padre*,' he said.

The two men smiled broadly at that, the two-gun man showing the gold in his mouth again. Whether Malpas's grammar was bad – he had intended to say 'it was my father's' – or his accent, he didn't know. Maybe they just felt like smiling. He extracted the Adams revolver slowly, set it on the table.

'*Cuchillo*?'

Had he any knives?

Malpas took the large clasp knife he carried out of his rocket and deposited that too.

'Come with me,' said the two-gun man.

II

It was an audience room, albeit a not very large one. At one end was a dais with an ornate chair on it; on this sat a small, fat man, much beringed and wearing a rather fancy *charro* suit. A much older man sat on a simple chair beside the dais. He wore a plain white shirt, and full cut dark trousers tucked into short riding-boots. He wore no rings. It was he who spoke.

'La pistola?'

'*Sin cartuchos, señor,*' said the two-gun man. No cartidges.

It was then that Malpas noticed something odd. There was dust on the old man's boots, as if he had just ridden in.

'You have a letter for me, *señor,*' said the man on the dais.

'You are Don Pablo Italico, sir?' Malpas asked. 'Mr Gaffney Sligo said I was to check.'

'I am. Chico here will confirm it.'

'*Es vero,*' said the two-gun man. Malpas didn't turn to glance at him but he could feel the smile.

'Then this is for you,' Malpas said as he approached nearer to the dais, handing over the letter. 'It is still sealed, sir.'

'Yes, it is and I know the seal,' Italico said. He took the letter and broke the seal.

Malpas knew exactly what the letter said. It was a command to Pablo Italico to hand over the person in his custody to the representative of Gaffney Sligo who presented it, all this over the signature of José Santiago. But Pablo de Italico was smiling as he read it and that meant something was badly wrong. It should worry him. It was unexpected but apparently genuine, bearing the signature and seal of Santiago. Malpas knew from past experience in the war what trouble sealed orders caused. Nobody ever smiled on receiving them.

'*Señor*,' Italico said, 'perhaps you would care to read this.' Thereupon he got out of his seat to pass the letter to the old man immediately beside the dais.

In that instant Malpas realized exactly what the true situation was. He went forward as if to take the letter himself. 'Sir, my orders are to let no one see that but you.'

Italico ignored him, as did the old man – a gringo's bad manners – but Malpas was now within a foot of the old man who was still intent on taking the letter from Italico. Malpas grabbed him by the shirt, swung him from his chair and in front of him, his left forearm over the skinny throat. He said softly, 'Italico, if you attack me I will break this man's neck. The same goes for your man Chico. And if anyone

112

cries out, the same.'

At the same time he was drawing the pistola using the old man's body to hide the fact. Finally it was in his hand and somehow he found the release hidden in the ornamentation, operated it and felt for the trigger it let fall. He had to move his grip forward, nearly dropped it, for he couldn't take his eyes off Chico who was standing frozen eight feet from him.

Chico saw the pistola. 'The gun is empty, *hombre*. Let the *caballero* go free and . . .' He was readying himself to draw, to fire at Malpas over the old man's head. He'd hit, too. Only his respect for the old man had held him back, Now his eyes were without doubt. Malpas raised the pistola and fired.

It was as if a bomb had gone off in his hand. He guessed later that the cruciform-cut bullet had broken in the barrel; all he saw then was Chico's belly erupt with blood as it ripped into him. The shock in his eyes was terrible, incredulous. He killed other men; no man killed Chico. But in an instant he was on his knees, his hands to his belly and blood gushing out between his fingers.

Malpas flung the old man forward at Chico,

diving forward himself, tearing the right-hand gun from Chico's holster.

He was only just in time. The one-gun killer was rushing towards him from the refectory – or whatever the table-room really was called – gun in hand. He saw the old man lying beside Chico, blood all over the pair of them, and froze. Malpas didn't, fanning the gun with his left hand, emptying the cylinder into him.

It was then that Pablo Italico made his move, coming from behind, knife in hand. Malpas heard him, half-turned, flung the empty gun at him, missing, but buying him time to get to his feet and meet the knife attack with his bare hands.

Pablo Italico was no knife fighter. In his position he'd never had to be, and the short, fancy-handled knife was for decoration rather than use, but it could kill. And sometimes amateurs got lucky.

He lunged forward. Malpas stepped back, pretended to stumble. Pablo Italico fell for it, came forward again, his arm bent, knife held as if to eat his dinner with. Malpas sidestepped, grasped the forearm and swung it and the knife back and up, impaling Italico on it. Then he flung him down to the floor. He never had much time for knife fighters, even amateur ones.

He gave himself half a second to take stock – four men down, three dead or dying, and not a shot fired except by himself. It was more than luck. He took two paces forward, caught the old man by his arm and hoisted him to his feet. He looked badly hurt, but the blood on his shirt wasn't his own. The blood was never his own.

'I don't seem to have a guide so you'll have to do, Santiago.'

The old man looked even more shocked at that. Malpas guessed he hadn't been called by his bare name, no *don* or *señor* before it, for the better part of a lifetime. He found himself unsympathetic.

'I am Don José de Santiago,' the old man said finally, not wholly without pride for all he was covered in blood and half stupefied with shock.

Malpas bent and retrieved the two guns still unfired and, holding one in each hand, hustled Santiago into the refectory. There on the table was his own Adams, which he slipped back into its holster, and the two shotgun shells. He left them. He wasn't going back into that charnel house. He hefted the two borrowed guns and said, 'Now, Santiago, take me to Miss Susan Hauksbee. No tricks or you'll get a bullet in each kidney.'

Santiago leaned on the table a moment as if unwell. 'You're a hard man, Malpas. It is Malpas, isn't it?'

'Yes.'

'You can have the girl. I'll take you to her but—'

'Do it now,' Malpas said and pushed the barrel of the left-hand gun in the general area of Santiago's left kidney.

They found Susan in a small parlour with three women. The shooting had already upset them and the sight of Malpas with his two guns and Santiago covered in blood sent them into hysterics. Susan alone kept her wits about her, but even she looked decidedly pale.

'Are you OK?' he asked.

She nodded.

'Then come on, we're leaving.'

Susan just stood there, looking at the hysterical women.

'Now,' Malpas snapped, and she started moving.

'Don't get between me and Santiago,' he said.

'I won't,' she agreed.

'Let's get to the horses.'

III

It was as if the nightmare had begun again. Maybe she'd thought of rescue, even dreamed Malpas would find her, but she had known it was just fantasy – and then it happened. But this was nothing like anything she'd imagined. He was so cold, so blood bespattered and utterly harsh. It was as if he had no time for her.

The courtyard was empty, but they found eight horses in the stables.

'Which is yours?' Malpas asked the old man in the bloody clothes, prodding him mercilessly with the guns he carried in either hand like a bandit.

'The Arab.'

'Saddle it for him,' he said to her as he examined the other horses. 'Two ridden recently beside the Arab. Those were your own guards. That leaves five, but one was surely the late Señor Italico's, so four *vaqueros* out there with guns. Where?'

That was no way to speak to an old man, whoever he was, but he answered for all that.

'In the *pueblo*, a *cantina* somewhere. I do not know precisely.' He paused. 'I didn't trust myself to Italico and his men. I was grossly in error, it seems.'

'Unlucky,' Malpas said, 'and very foolish to play that charade with me. Italico gave it away.'

'I chose poor men.'

'No, Santiago, either of them could have killed me if you hadn't been there. They were terrified of hurting you . . . so they froze up.'

She finished cinching the saddle on the Arab, a lovely horse, then watched with horror as Malpas stripped the lariat from its saddle and made a noose and slipped it around the old man's neck.

'Now, mount up but keep close if you don't want to get dry hung.'

Malpas tied off the other end to the saddle-horn of his sorrel, loosed its reins from the hitching rail and walked it to the north-facing gate, slipped the bar off it and pulled it open. 'Ride out on my left,' he said to her. 'If I get shot just ride north – and ride like hell.'

'But Jack—'

'Don't argue, do exactly as I say.' Then he looked to Santiago who was mounted now and controlling his fidgety horse; the slack of the lariat looped on the ground behind him.

Susan mounted the remaining sorrel and rode forward, keeping to Jack Malpas's left. As she did so she couldn't help noticing he'd stuck the two spare guns in his belt; the result was to make him look quite piratical. Except she knew now there was no glamour at all in the way pirates behaved.

There were few houses on the northern side and they rode quickly and saw no one. She had difficulty keeping up with Malpas; the old man on the Arab didn't but then he had good reason not to and the Arab was obviously fleeter than either of the two sorrels. Then they were past the last of the houses and out on the scrubland.

She wanted to ride up close to Malpas and talk to him, to have him talk to her, and she found herself wishing she were a better horse-woman. She'd ridden back East, but it was different here and she hadn't gotten back into the Western style.

And then the full realization dawned on her,

somewhat belatedly: she was free. They were free and clear. The nightmare was consigned to the past. And Jack Malpas had saved her. Brutally, but maybe it had been the only way. She glanced at his face, then looked away. There was something terrible about his aspect, an absolute implacability. Yet she was certain that underneath it all there was something more.

'Keep up!' he yelled back at her.

IV

Malpas knew they were being followed after just a few minutes from starting out. He felt it and it was confirmed when he turned in the saddle and saw the four figures, maybe five hundred yards back but making good time.

He should have shot the other horses, he thought, but Susan had been there; there could have been other horses in the pueblo. And he liked horses. . . . No, there were some things you just didn't do, but it meant he'd have to fight again and that was pushing the odds.

He'd been very lucky indeed, partly because

Santiago and Italico thought to have some fun with him. But now the pistola trick was all used up, and anyway that second gunman should have taken him, but the sight of his master, Santiago, all covered with blood had shaken the gunman and so saved him. What would now?

The horses were slowing as they came to the rise. 'Faster!' he yelled, applying the spur and was pleased to see Susan keeping up with him. Santiago, at the end of the lariat, he didn't need to worry about.

Forty yards beyond the ridge they were just out of sight of their pursuers. He called a halt, being careful with Santiago this time. He was still an ace card.

'Get down, *hombre*,' he snapped. Had Santiago ever been called plain 'man' before? But he got down. Malpas quickly loosed the lariat from his saddlehorn and used it to bind him, talking to Susan Hauksbee as he did so. 'Susan, hold the horses here. *Hold* them. If I get killed, get on the Arab and make for home. But I won't.'

'What are you going to do?'

'Delay our pursuers a little,' he said and ran back to near the top of the rise; bending low he moved to the very edge and laid himself down on the hot earth, after setting both the borrowed guns beside him. He left the Adams in its holster.

They were two hundred yards off, less maybe. Careful men would have split up, made less of a target of themselves, but they'd seen the dead men in Casa del Norte and they were hot for vengeance.

He took a deep breath. This was his one chance. They obviously hadn't seen him here but they knew they were chasing just one armed man so they weren't afraid. They were probably no worse horsemen than he and maybe better. Their horses were certainly fresher. For a moment he wished for a rifle but truth to tell he'd never been all that good with a rifle. He'd had little practice. Town marshals don't fight at long range and in the army he'd been an officer with a handgun.

A hundred yards. The temptation to draw a bead and fire was almost overwhelming but he resisted it. A handgun bullet would carry that far easily but aimed shots were impossible. He waited, then at fifty yards he picked up one of the borrowed guns and fanned the six bullets in it at the oncoming men and horses.

The grouping helped him. Instead of spreading out they'd bunched up, making in effect a large target. One man went down, knocked off his horse as if by a giant hand. The rest came on.

Malpas fired the second handgun, fanning again at a range of less than thirty yards. They were firing back but he disregarded that – nobody hit anything they aimed at from the back of a galloping horse.

Now, two more horses and men were down and only one came on – and the rider seemingly hadn't spotted him! He broke over the ridge ten yards to Malpas's right, one hand holding the reins, one holding a Colt 1850 which he was working furiously, firing forward.

Malpas dropped the empty gun from his hand, rose and drew the Adams at the same time. He put three bullets into the rider. The terrified horse bolted, its dead rider slumped over its neck, and there was nobody left before or behind him. Whether the men on the felled horses were dead or just wounded didn't matter; they were *hors de combat.*

But the last man had fired wildly. He looked back, saw Susan was uninjured. He drew breath. But one of the sorrels was down – and

123

where was Santiago?

He ran over, holstering his gun as he did so. 'Are you OK?'

'It fell on him, the horse fell on him!' She was almost hysterical.

The head-shot horse had indeed fallen upon Santiago, fully across his belly and chest. Malpas knelt down and put his hand to Santiago's neck, searching out the carotid artery. Nothing. Then he looked at the eyes, glazed with death. He didn't close them.

But there was something around the neck he hadn't seen before, a piece of twine. He pulled on it and found a ring hung around the neck, his seal ring. Of course – the charade. If Santiago had worn his seal ring it would have been obvious who he was. At least to a Mexican. In the circumstances Malpas knew he might not have noticed. He tossed the ring in the air, then slipped it into his pocket. Flynn might like it as a memento. He stood up. 'He's dead, his chest is crushed.'

He could see she was close to tears. 'He was José de Santiago, the man who had you kidnapped. He'd come to see you and gloat. He was going to—'

'Please stop!' she said, and there were tears

in her eyes now. 'We must . . .' She broke off.

What? Bury him? Malpas held his temper. She was distraught; too much had happened to her; to many men had died around her. He reached out to touch her arm.

She shied away.

Hurt, Malpas was silent a moment, then he said, 'Mount up, you're going home. I'll take the Arab.'

'Do we just leave him. . . ?'

Malpas lost his temper at last. 'Hell, woman, this is a battlefield. Get mounted.'

EIGHT

I

Malpas rode north-west over land that was edging from scrub to grass. He thought, why not turn this pleasant ride into a real one, ride north until he came to a railroad that could take him on to California? What would he be leaving behind? A few items in his hotel room, all easily replaceable, and that was about it.

Even his hotel bill was paid. If it hadn't been, he would have had difficulty paying it. He hadn't been able to pay for a drink, a cigar or a meal for the last two days. He was the hero who had saved Susan Hauksbee and spat in the eye of the Santiagos who had kept the border closed to trade.

He needn't even go to California. There wasn't a town in the West which wouldn't appoint him town marshal if he asked for the job, such would be his rep' when the news spread.

But he'd never wear a badge or star again. A marshal had to believe in his luck and a man had to know when not to push it too far. He hadn't just won against the odds at Casa del Norte. When things went sour he should have had no chance at all. So why was he still here?

He stroked his horse's neck. The Arab was a magnificent animal, not a tall horse but fleet and strong and full of heart. Which was more than Santiago, Italico and their men had been. Of course, Santiago hadn't trusted Italico and so had sent the latter's guards away, unwittingly reducing the odds down to two to one. And even when he had the upper hand, Santiago couldn't resist playing a lordly game – a game that let his enemy near him.

Malpas didn't doubt that Chico and his partner had been quick draws, fast and deadly, but they'd been paralysed by the risk to Santiago and something more; they hadn't truly expected him to fight back. As for Italico's men, they'd chased him like hunters after a fox, but he hadn't been a fox, he'd been a wolf, and they'd paid for their misjudgement. All in all, it had been a house of cards.

That admitted, he'd still been damnably lucky, so why the taste of bile in his mouth?

The question scarcely needed answering. On the long, uneventful ride back to San Geronimo, she'd been as cold as ice. He'd told her about Gaffney Sligo, Polvertown, everything, and she'd said nothing. Even the hysteria had been better. He guessed she'd been overwhelmed by the brutality of it all and blamed him. And now she was ensconced in her ranch house and no word from her in two days.

Leave it, he thought. He'd got what he wanted from San Geronimo – his life back. He'd only stayed because of the meeting on the stage with an 'emancipated young woman' with a taste for bad poetry.

Turn north?

Almost despite himself, he found he was turning the Arab stallion back to the southeast.

II

Susan Hauksbee, sitting by her bedroom window, saw the rider half a mile off. She closed her copy of Byron's *The Giaour*, setting it atop her leather-bound *Marmion*, stood up and walked over to her dressing-table.

Nothing looked different in the mirror. She was still the same girl who had ridden into San Geronimo only days ago on the stage; no lines, no grey hair, not even circles under the eyes from weeping which she'd done a lot of in the last two days.

She considered brushing her hair but it didn't need it so she turned for the door. Flynn was too old a friend to keep waiting.

'You'll lose him if you're not careful,' Flynn said, trying to handle the ridiculously small china cup she'd brought back from the East. The handle especially seemed to be made for midgets.

'He's not mine to lose,' she said.

Flynn replaced the cup on its saucer. It wasn't an answer at all, just a retort, but he knew he'd been answered fully nonetheless. She didn't want him to leave. 'So no more notes for him?' he asked, trying a little subtlety himself.

She drank her coffee, considering. 'Perhaps I really ought to thank him formally.'

Flynn lost patience with the game. 'Formally!' he snapped. 'Do you know what would have happened to you if he hadn't risked his life for you?'

She didn't reply, so Malpas must have been too gentle, only hinted at it. Flynn was much more precise and saw her go white. He still didn't stop. 'Did he tell you how he planned it?' He took out the seal ring Malpas had given him. 'Did he tell you how it was sealed with this ring, only not quite?'

'Tell me,' she said.

Flynn did, telling exactly how Gaffney Sligo's name had been used, his part in it all. He concluded, 'I reckon Malpas had a one in three chance of getting you away if the letter was accepted as genuine. If not, no chance at all. Do you think he didn't know the odds when he set off?'

'Of course not,' she said, much abashed.

But she was still angry with him, Flynn saw. She had her head stuffed with romantic dreams and couldn't see the reality behind them when it was set before her. They didn't teach reality, red in tooth and claw, back in the

New England finishing-schools.

'He's a good man,' he said, not knowing what more he could say. 'He can be a marshal again wherever he chooses.'

'He couldn't before?'

'No. He'd been badly shot up and left full of fever. That's why he crossed the Little Stony. Kill or cure, I guess. But it didn't cure his crippled hand.'

'What are you talking about?'

So she hadn't known. He told her what Squire had told him, finishing off his coffee as she gave way finally to tears. Suddenly he laughed.

She wiped her eyes. 'Are you laughing at me?' she asked with the beginnings of anger in her voice. 'I—'

'Not at you, at myself. Here I am like an old fool, playing cupid for all I'm worth, but you'd never any intention of letting him go.' Or he you, he thought, but he didn't say it.

'What do you mean?'

Flynn decided on a little subtlety himself. 'Do you know, he offered me the Arab as replacement for the dead sorrel. I didn't accept, of course.' He paused. 'He rides it every day.'

'Not here,' she said.

'He hasn't had a formal invitation,' Flynn said. 'Maybe you should write him one now.'

III

'He's a magnificent beast,' Anders Flynn said, admiring the Arab now eating oats in a stall in his barn. From the slightly regretful tone he employed, Malpas guessed he knew that his father had turned down accepting the horse. Malpas took no offence at that regret. The Arab was a horse breeder's dream.

'You worried about Susan?' Flynn persisted.

'She's safe,' Malpas said.

'She's sulking. So Pa says and he's usually right. Women do sulk. My Sonya does. Hell, it's a miracle we get along, but we do. Know how we met?'

'No.'

'It's a long story but I'll keep it short. My ma came from Minnesota. Her pa lost his farm, came down here prospecting. Never found no gold and he broke his neck trying. Ma was working as a cook on the Hauksbee spread 'fore Pa married her.' He took breath, just.

132

'Well, she kept in touch with her folks back in Minnesota by letter and Sonya, who's Cousin Jacobsen's kid, would add a postscript to all the letters. So Ma got me to write a postscript likewise and we got to know each other. Then, when I was eighteen, Ma took herself off to Minnesota and brought Sonya back and we hit it off. Ma died the year after. Now ain't that romantic?'

No, Malpas thought, but he nodded anyway. He'd met Sonya when he arrived at the ranch, a buxom, flaxen haired woman of about thirty with two kids pulling at her apron and a Minnesota accent you could cut with a knife. He'd liked her instantly.

'You reckon there'll be any comeback from the Santiagos?'

'No,' Malpas said. 'They'll be too busy fighting amongst themselves to succeed him. The kidnapping is now an embarrassment. Any more trouble and they risk bringing in the US government and that would get them in hot water with Mexico City.'

'Yeah, I reckon you're right. When you're in the wrong you keep your head down.'

'You do at that,' Malpas said, thinking of Gaffney Sligo who'd done exactly that. Who could now believe that Josiah Polver had been in on the kidnapping – with José Santiago! So it was infinitely better for Sligo if the matter was never raised. Malpas had intended to charge Santiago with kidnapping and bring him to a US court, but chance had precluded that. A dead man couldn't testify, only a living one. And without Santiago there was no evidence implicating Sligo, only speculation. And suddenly he knew what he had to do.

'What about that dinner you promised me – will it be ready yet?'

'If it isn't, I can offer you a glass of something while you wait,' Anders Flynn said, clapping him on the back.

It was two hours later before Juan Flynn arrived back from the Hauksbee ranch. Night was falling and the children were being put to bed. His son, Anders, poured a drink for him and clapped him on the back too. 'Couldn't wait dinner, Pa. We have a guest.'

'I can see that, you great drunken lummox,' his father said amiably. 'You've got him drunk too?'

'I ain't drunk, Pa. It takes two bottles of aquavit to get me drunk,' Anders said.

'We shared the one bottle,' Malpas said. 'And Sonya had a glass too. She deserved no less for her fine cookery.'

'Danish,' Anders said. 'She gave us *rødgrød med fløde* to finish. She left you some for later, Pa.'

Juan Flynn smiled. 'Go kiss my grandchildren goodnight. I need to speak with Marshal Malpas alone.'

'Sure thing,' Anders said, departing.

'Fine boy,' his father said, smiling after him. 'Takes after his mother.'

'You've been to see Susan,' Malpas said.

'Yes, I have a note from her for you.' He took an envelope out of his pocket end gave it to him. Malpas opened it and read:

Dear Jack,

Please feel free to visit the Hauksbee ranch at any time so I may thank you for your great kindness.

　　Sincerely,
　　　Susan.

'You know what it says?'

'Of course.' He paused. 'She was in tears as she wrote it.' He didn't add that its brevity was at least partly down to his own impatience.

'She saw too much,' Malpas said.

'You'll go?'

'In due time,' Malpas said. 'First, tell me who owns the newspaper now.'

'She does, but I manage it. I have power of attorney. Her uncle had it before, but after his death she confirmed it to me by telegraph. That'll pass in our courts.'

'So you could sell it to me?'

'Technically, yes.'

'So how much is it worth?'

Flynn considered, this. 'It doesn't make a profit but the fitments are probably worth a thousand dollars.'

'I'll buy it.'

'She could challenge the sale—'

'If she chooses to, no problem. She can buy it back. But it's better if I own it.'

'For her protection.'

Malpas nodded. 'I'll need to get out an edition. Is one already set up?'

'Nearly. Most of the stories are a touch old.'

'I don't care about that. Just the first page.'

'If Gaffney Sligo sues, you won't stand a

chance in court, hero or not,' Juan Flynn said, in no doubt as to the nature of the story that Malpas intended to publish.

'If the paper's in my name at least he can't touch the Hauksbee ranch. But I doubt he'll sue. He can't be sure what I know, what I learnt in Mexico. And obviously I'll hint at such proofs.'

'Maybe. It would still leave him one other option.'

'To call me out.'

'And are you sure you'd win?'

Malpas shrugged. 'I've faced men before. I came through. Maybe one day I won't. But I have to try. If Gaffney Sligo's let be, he'll win even now. Susan can't stand up to him any more than Polver could. But in this he's isolated. His men won't follow him if they think he sold an American girl to a Mexican. He'll have to clear himself and that's the obvious way.'

'You should tell her first.'

'After's better. Less tears.'

Flynn took his time in answering, 'Yes, you're right. We haven't beaten Gaffney Sligo. But he's fast.'

'There's more to it than that,' Malpas said. 'I

reckon Gaffney Sligo is another little tin god like Santiago. He's always had men to back him. He'll be on his own on Main Street.'

'God help me if you're wrong,' Flynn said. 'She'll never speak to me again.'

'Neither will I,' Malpas said. 'Draw up the bill of sale.'

NINE

I

Crystalman was worried. 'Jack, you should have come to me.' He was holding a copy of the *Gazette* which boldly announced:

GAFFNEY SLIGO ACCUSED

This journal can now reveal that Mr Jack Malpas, the respected former town marshal of Coopersville, has alleged that local rancher Mr Gaffney Sligo was implicated in the kidnapping of Miss Susan Hauksbee by the late José Santiago.

'Why?' Malpas asked.

'So I could lay charges.'

'Lay them now,' Malpas said. 'Take a few more copies if you wish, free, gratis.' He gestured at the pile of copies on the newspaper office counter. 'Or you could send for a Federal marshal. He might bring up the business at Polvertown though.'

Crystalman suddenly looked very uncomfortable. He said, 'Well, maybe it's a civil matter. He can sue you for libel.'

Malpas smiled. 'You think so?'

'No, my guess is he'll call you out.'

'And what will you do about that?'

'I could post you both out of town, but then I'd have to enforce it. You were always quicker than me, Jack, and he's got twenty men behind him.' Sam Crystalman sighed. 'I'll do nothing.' He paused, glanced back at the headline. 'It's true, ain't it?'

'Yeah.'

'The whole town half-believes it already, but that'll change if he kills you. He'll own the town then.'

'He doesn't now?'

'No,' Crystalman said, a little too quickly. 'OK, so I went to Polvertown but then so did you, and I was never in his pocket. Hell, he

140

didn't need no favours. And he'll get none now. I ain't got no time for a man who'll sell a lady to the likes of Santiago.'

'I believe you, Sam.'

'Then believe this. He's fast and he's accurate and, given the chance, he'll empty his gun into you. I heard tell he killed a man some years back supposedly caught stealing on his ranch. Maybe he was, maybe not, but he gave him a chance: go to jail or draw. The fella decided to risk the draw. The tale is that Sligo came up close, damn near blew him apart and laughed afterwards. Watch yourself, Jack.' And with that, Sam Crystalman left. He didn't take any further copies of the *Gazette* with him.

So the law was squared, Malpas thought. It was up to Gaffney Sligo now: shoot it out or sue. All he had to do was wait, and here was as good a place as any. He leant on the counter and lit a cigar.

'Do you need some help?' Susan asked.

Malpas looked up, saw her standing at the door in a grey silk dress that brought out the colour of her eyes.

'Situations do seem to be reversed,' he said. 'But I've already had help. Flynn worked through the night and got the copies out. He wouldn't let me do much.'

'Why should you? You're the new proprietor, so I hear.'

'It's legal.'

'I don't at all care about that, Jack. I know why you and Flynn did it but . . .' She broke off. 'I'm sorry I was so stupid. It was just all so horrible and—'

'And I was harsh and hard. Maybe you should remember that. I sometimes am.'

She smiled. 'The people who really are never admit to it.' She paused. 'Isn't there some way . . .'

'I can't back down,' Malpas said.

'I know,' she said, and he saw she was holding back tears. She went on, 'I didn't come to argue with you, Jack. I just had to be here.'

'You're very welcome,' Malpas said.

II

. . . Mr Malpas states that he has in his possession incontrovertible proof that he will in due time reveal to the prosecuting authorities . . .

142

Gaffney Sligo set the paper down on the polished mahogany table by the window of his elegant parlour.

'What do you reckon, Gaff?' asked Ken Rivers who'd ridden out to the ranch with the *Gazette*. 'It sounds bad.'

Sligo glanced up at him, saw Rivers was worried but not too worried. After all, his name hadn't been mentioned.

'It's just talk,' Sligo said, leaning back on his chair. 'If he had proof he'd say straight out what it was.'

'Yeah, I reckon you're right. All the same . . .'

Gaffney Sligo sighed. That was exactly right – all the same . . . Whatever forum it was made in, paper or court, such a charge had to be answered. And quickly. Santiago's men hadn't crossed the border to take the Hauksbee girl because it was safer that way – it wasn't – but because it was something virtually all of his own men wouldn't go for, or stay by him if they knew of it.

Still, that was no problem yet. A simple denial would serve to keep the cowhands loyal. But they'd expect him to do something.

Sue? It was exceptionally tempting. Malpas

was by all accounts an honest lawman so there'd be no money there, but the paper was a Hauksbee property. He might well end with the ranch in lieu of damages.

And what evidence could they have? Ken Rivers had been the go-between and he wouldn't talk. Sligo had a strong hold over him; he was wanted for a murder in Kansas. And there'd been no incriminating letters, that at Santiago's insistence. Even the gambling markers had been returned once the Hauksbee girl had been taken. So there was no reason at all not to sue.

'You mind, Gaff?'

'No, pour yourself one,' Sligo said.

'Thanks,' Rivers said, going over to the drinks cabinet and helping himself to a tumblerfull of bourbon. There was imported malt whisky there too but Rivers would never even consider that.

'Damn it, I needed that!' Rivers said, pouring himself a second. 'It had me worried.'

It took a lot to worry Rivers, who was as stupid as a man could be and still be a good cowhand. 'Don't drink too much,' Sligo said. 'You've work to do.'

'No,' Rivers said. 'She paid me off late yesterday – a full month's wages. That's how I got the paper. I stayed in town last night.'

'Did she say why?'

'Just that she'd be running things from now on.' He poured a third glass. 'Do you reckon I can stay on here?'

'Sure,' Sligo said. Did she know about Rivers's part? No, she had to be just guessing. It didn't alter anything. Except she'd done it herself and reminded him that if he sued he'd be up against her in court. Malpas was a stranger out of Texas, the hero of the hour but hours pass quickly; she was and would remain the Hauksbee girl from these parts who'd been badly wronged. They'd give her the benefit of any doubt they could find, reasonable or otherwise.

He was certain she'd no proof, nor Malpas either, but what if she lied? He'd been assuming she was too much the lady for that but a lady was just a woman with airs and graces. They could be dispensed with at need.

No, he couldn't risk the courts. But he'd really known that from the beginning. There was only one way. He'd have to challenge Malpas. 'Damn it to hell!' he said.

'Do you want a drink, Gaff?'

'No, not now. I'm going to town.'

'Yeah, I reckoned you would. Folks kinda expect it. And I hear tell this Malpas fella's got a bad right hand, needs a fancy double-action pistol, though it didn't stop him from killing them greasers. But maybe he backshot 'em. Talk is that he took the Butler gang with a shotgun.' Rivers finished off his third glass. 'It's easy for a marshal to get a big rep' when he can use a Greener. But he ain't a marshal now. And I never seen nobody faster than you, Gaff.'

Sligo smiled. He knew Rivers wasn't simply flattering him. He'd worked at being fast and he'd four notches on his gun to prove it. And this wouldn't be just the fifth notch; he'd inherit Malpas's whole rep'. Nobody would dare to cross him. And a woman alone couldn't run a ranch. He'd end up with it. In fact, he'd end up owning San Geronimo.

'Want me to come along?'

Sligo was about to say no, then stopped himself. Perhaps he'd underestimated the danger Ken Rivers posed to him. Even very stupid men talked in their cups. He needed dealing with; he was certainly precious little use to him now he was no longer the

146

Hauksbee foreman.

Or maybe not quite. Despite the drink he'd taken, there was no slurring in Rivers's voice and Sligo knew that the same would apply to his aim.

'Why not?' he said. 'If you care to even the odds. . . .'

Rivers smiled. 'Sure, Gaff. I know just what to do.'

Gaffney Sligo smiled too. However things turned out, the town would take Rivers for a Hauksbee man.

'Let's ride,' he said. All he had to do to win was to kill one man: Jack Malpas!

III

It was almost noon when Flynn came back. He found Malpas sitting behind the counter while Susan was wearing one of the aprons and breaking up set type for re-use.

'You'll get oil on your dress.'

She just smiled. He realized that she needed to be doing something, anything. All the more so now, he thought as he said, 'He's out there, in Main Street.'

'Any men with him?'

'Two, but Crystalman took their guns off them. I was surprised.'

'I had my doubts, too, but I was wrong. He's an honest lawman.'

'He didn't take Gaffney Sligo's.'

'He couldn't do that,' Malpas replied. 'This thing has to be settled. We all know that.' He stood up, walked out from behind the counter.

'Jack. . . .'

Malpas stopped, turned.

'Come back safe,' she said.

He just nodded and walked out of the office.

Flynn looked at her. He could see no tears now. 'Are you—'

'I'll stay here,' she said.

Flynn hesitated, torn, then he, too, turned and left.

IV

Malpas had begun the business in a cold anger but the anger was gone now, though not the coldness. It was just a job, like dealing with the bank robbers in Coopersville, though the odds were better.

He went the long way round into Main Street. Let Gaffney Sligo see him coming, let the fear build up in him.

When he did step out onto the otherwise empty street, he saw Sligo sixty yards away, standing by the hotel, waiting. He was wearing a grey suit, the right side of his coat pulled back to reveal a six-gun, tied down across his thigh. He was drawing attention to it, Malpas thought, as if to say this is all you have to worry about. He would have a second gun.

Malpas slipped off his own coat, dropped it in the dirt. If he were shot there'd be less material to be carried into the wound.

Fifty yards. Just keep walking, Sligo wouldn't fire at this range; nobody would. He hadn't even starting walking yet. That, too, was to the good. Better to be doing something.

Forty yards. Sligo started off. Not long now. This was harder than he remembered. Drawing, firing back – that was easy. The waiting was hard.

Thirty yards, long shooting distance, but Sligo was just coming on. Was his face more florid than usual?

'Jack!'

Malpas flicked his eyes to the left, saw Susan

in the street that led straight to the newspaper office. She'd come out after all, but now she was running towards a man at the corner and he saw why. He was one of the men he'd seen in the Polvertown business, Ken Rivers, the Hauksbee foreman, and he had a gun drawn and in his hand. But now Susan was on him, grasping after the gun. He pushed her away brutally. She fell.

Without thinking, Malpas drew and fired. The man fell, firing himself, the bullet lost in the dirt of the roadway.

It took all his will power to temporarily put her out of mind and keep on walking, gun in hand now, towards Gaffney Sligo. He daren't turn and be shot in the back.

Gaffney Sligo stopped, drew and fired. At over twenty yards, but it was a good shot. Malpas felt a stinging in his upper right arm which rapidly spread throughout the arm. He almost dropped his gun.

But not quite. He'd only been creased. He started firing himself, just pulling the trigger and letting it cock itself, which no longer felt odd, and then saw Sligo had been hit.

Malpas saw the gun fall from Sligo's hand. He held his fire, waiting. It was a trick, as he'd guessed. Sligo's other arm jerked out, towards him.

From ten yards Malpas emptied the cylinder into him, saw the big man jerk under the blows, then fall face-down in the dirt.

Malpas walked right up to him, kicked the six-gun aside. And then he looked to Sligo's left sleeve protruding from which was a cord, which itself was fastened to a derringer lying inches away from his hand. He'd guessed right, a second gun.

A mistake. Sligo had given himself too much to think about. Even the back shooting attempt had been a mistake. He holstered the Adams. Gaffney Sligo had been fast, very fast. If he had played it straight. . . .

'Derringer!' Sam Crystalman exclaimed. He'd suddenly come out from somewhere and was standing over the body. He bent, ripped the holdout gun free, made sure it wasn't cocked and tossed it over.

Malpas caught it with his right, examined it, broke it open and let the cartridges fall. And then it struck him his thumb was working again. Now he didn't need it desperately, now Sligo was dead, it was working.

He let out his breath. It was over. The empty

street was now bustling with people. He turned, saw Susan standing in the middle of the alley, Flynn supporting her.

'Justifiable homicide,' Crystalman shouted. 'Somebody get the undertaker. I want this back-shooting scum off Main Street.'

But Malpas was no longer listening. He was running back in the direction of the newspaper office.

EPILOGUE

Malpas drove the buggy up to the hitching rail of the Hauksbee ranch house, having inspected the house thoroughly for the last half mile. It was a timber-frame building, not very large, probably six bedroomed, with a pleasant veranda. All in all, pretty modern for these parts where most ranch houses were simple adobe buildings. The bunkhouse here was exactly that, an old Mexican building, but the barn was huge and timber framed too, and the corrals were in good order though empty at the moment. He climbed out of the buggy, hitched the horse and went back to help Susan out.

She still looked pretty groggy, not all the

street dirt off her grey dress nor quite washed off her face either. The only pristine thing about her was the fine white sling about her right arm.

'There we go,' he said as she stepped on to the veranda.

'I'm not a horse,' she said.

Involuntarily, Malpas looked to the horse tied up before the buggy, decided it was safe for the moment.

Susan noticed. 'Are you coming inside?'

'I'm not sure I ought to,' he said. 'There doesn't seem to be anybody about to chaperon you.'

'They all went to town to watch the gunfight,' she said, adding snappily, 'and as for a chaperon, this will do quite well.' She moved her right arm a little by way of illustration and grimaced at the result.

Malpas made no reply but opened the door for her and followed her in. The vestibule led to a parlour of quite unfeminine unclutteredness, with leather-covered chairs and sofa and a table made for use; it was decorated only by a single oil painting hung where it was out of direct sunlight. The shadow suited it. It was a poorly painted portrait of an old man in his

Sunday best with a long rifle in his hand and a steer to one side. Whether he was about to shoot the animal was unclear.

'My father,' Susan said, noticing his glance. 'This was his favourite room. The painting was done locally.'

'A good likeness?' he asked politely.

'It's the only one I have,' she said. 'Won't you sit down?'

Malpas sat down on the sofa. She took one of the chairs. 'Your hand's better,' she said.

Malpas nodded. 'I could go back to marshalling if I wanted to.'

'And do you?' A touch of tightness in her voice.

'No. I've pushed my luck far enough in that direction.'

'So what then?'

Malpas lost patience, mostly with himself. He stood up. 'You know why I'm here. Shall we give it a go?'

'Give what a go?' she asked.

'I'm asking you to marry me.'

'We scarcely know each other,' she said.

'Doc Litton said the sprain should be better in a week or so. We can put off the ceremony till then. That would give us time.'

She stood up too. 'That's probably long enough,' she agreed, and a moment later was in his arms.